ONE TOO MANY

Find the author at
johnherndonauthor.com.

One Too Many

A Novel

John Herndon

Off The Books Press
Austin MMXVI

ISBN-10 1523359056
ISBN-13 978-1523359059

First Print Edition, Paperback, January 2016
Off The Books Press

Also published as an ebook in January 2016.

10 9 8 7 6 5 4 3 2 1

Acknowledgments:
Cover art: Matthew Bivalacqua
Book design: Victoria Champion (Luminous Points Publishing)

Thanks:
Joe Ahearn, Robert Bogan, Robert Bonazzi, Deanna Brochin, Richard Price, Christina Puentes, Timeca Seretti, Drew Thomas, Gary Kent

To My Sons

1

The nicest thing about Austin, Texas is the neighborhoods.

No doubt you've heard Austin is a party town, with all the music, food and celebrities, Sixth Street, South by Southwest, ACL Fest, Formula I, etc., and it's all true.

But the best thing about Austin is the neighborhoods, and the best thing about the neighborhoods is they're so quiet.

I lived in North Austin just a couple of blocks from the demographic center of the entire metropolitan area, and sometimes it was so quiet that the cooing of the doves was the loudest sound. The dogs didn't bother to bark at the mailman. The cats spent most of their time sleeping.

Austin grew up as a college town, and had the shady, tree-lined streets that went with that heritage. My neighbors and I grew all kinds of pretty flowers. Many of us, faced with the on-going drought, were moving away from the traditional lawns that have to be watered and mowed toward xeriscaping with native trees, grasses, cactus and wildflowers.

Since I worked hard, invested wisely and got lucky, I was able to retire at 35. I quit the rat race and bought my house here and bit by bit converted my lawn to buffalo grass, big and little bluestem and eastern gama grass; I had several patches of bluebonnets, Indian blanket and Mexican hat; trails of crushed granite wound among bunches of prickly pear and agave.

So like I said, the best thing about Austin neighborhoods was they were so quiet. The only problem was, it was too damn quiet.

2

I was able to make my fortune and retire by working diligently at that most quintessential of American enterprises—armed robbery.

"Some will rob you with a six gun, and some with a fountain pen," according to Woodie Guthrie. And I'm here to guarantee you that the one with the pen will make a whole lot more money. I fell somewhere in between.

Armed robbery, in particular bank robbery, is not especially complicated or strenuous. The most important personal quality called for is self-control. Most people simply aren't capable of the level of self-control required, or more people would take up robbery as a profession.

I seem to have been born with a greater degree of self-control than the vast majority of people. At least, that's what they tell me.

My father was a doctor in a small town. He did all right but never made a lot of money. My mom was Catholic, so they had a lot of children; I was the last of six, and there are seven years and some months between me and my youngest sister. Growing up, I was like an only child. When I was in first grade my sister was starting high school. Two of my brothers were married and had kids of their own. I wonder if I may have gotten some of my self-assurance from my upbringing; I was always surrounded by adults. But they all say I was my own man from a very early age. I was never a mama's boy; I was always her little man. No one paid much attention to me; I was mostly left to my own devices.

In high school, I learned the value of self-control. I was hanging out at a friend's house whose parents were out of town. This was back in Florida. There were kids all around the swimming pool and a fair amount of booze and smoke and a little blow; everyone was pretty high. This other friend Jake and I and a couple of chicks wandered out onto the golf course and started making out on the 13th green. Suddenly this asshole Bennett from school showed up with his crew. He started giving Jake a bunch of shit about some bad coke he sold him, and the next thing he pulled out a piece and threw down on him all gangster style. The girls were screaming and the crew were cussing but I was standing right there when he flashed that gun and I just snatched it out of his hand and slapped him across the nose with the barrel. He gasped and dropped to his knees. He was crying like a little girl. Blood was running everywhere. Jake was standing there with his mouth hanging open. The crew started charging but I waved that pistol at them and they backed off fast. I told them to help Bennett up and to get the fuck out of there. When they were out of sight I threw the gun into the canal and we went back to the party like nothing had happened. I got laid that night.

After that, Jake always took me along when he was doing deals, and always cut me in. Word got around pretty fast. Nobody ever fucked with me.

By the time I graduated high school, my parents were pretty well played out. They held on while I finished my degree in psychology, but then my dad died and my mom too pretty soon after that. They owned their own home and some stocks and all that, but they loved all their kids exactly the same amount, and so they divided their assets six ways exactly. That left me with a little less than $25,000. I'm not saying it wasn't fair. But $25,000 was a far different matter to my brother the lawyer and my brother the doctor than it was to me.

A lot of people disparage a liberal arts degree, but I learned a lot in my psychology courses—about myself. I learned some of the sources of my self-control. I learned that I needed intellectual freedom and freedom of action. I could never work for a boss in an office. I needed something that would afford me a living and provide a challenge and stimulus, a little excitement. I knew it wasn't going to be counseling the mentally disturbed. I had another idea how I could put that psychology degree to work.

Now my father's people were pretty well behaved, pretty prim and proper. But on my mother's side, there was Uncle Bill, her half-brother or step-brother or something. He wasn't a con man exactly, but he was a pretty sharp operator, and some of the corners he cut landed him in prison for a short stay a couple of different times. While he was there, he made contacts. Uncle Bill had an image to maintain. He was always wooing wealthy widows or other investors and he had to look the part. He wouldn't dirty his hands. But he knew people.

So I told him I wanted to meet someone. He looked at me with a sort of half-smile. "You sure you know what you're getting yourself into?" he said.

"I want to make my own way. I just need a chance to get some experience."

So he gave me a name. I got my start.

When the cops say that 95 percent of criminals are really, really dumb, they're right. Most don't have the IQ god gave a chicken. Many are downright despicable. No doubt the human race would be a lot better off if most of them were killed before they could reproduce.

Then there's the other five percent.

The criminal life actually draws more than its share of geniuses and near geniuses. I wouldn't claim to be either, but I've met a few.

As I mentioned earlier, it doesn't take a genius to rob a bank. There are guys who prove that every day. Robbing the bank's the easy part. Most guys rob the bank and go straight to jail. To do it right, you have to be smart.

The first thing you have to know is the right financial institution to rob. You can only get this information from a fence. Fences of course work both ways—buying stolen goods, and setting up the robberies in advance. The fences are some of the most powerful, intelligent and creative people in the industry. Some of them are legendary.

Someone high up in the bank or whatever has to be in on the deal. That's the only way to get the information, and that's the fence's special talent—finding these guys. They way over-report the amount of cash they have on hand, of course. There's always ridiculous insurance and someone at the insurance company has to be greased. This all takes weeks and even months to set up.

You're a contractor. So you get your lead and you head to the location. I never took jobs in my home state, wherever that might be—I always moved around a lot. I always liked to drive. Even better if the place was two, three states away. Say I was living in Denver and the gig was in Memphis. That was about perfect for me. I got to see this great country and get to know the deluded American sheeple, who think themselves as gentle as lambs when they're really quite wolfish.

I always drove a Toyota Camry, probably the most invisible car in America, two to six years old. I gave myself plenty of time. I never got in a hurry. I always took four or five identities along for emergencies. I'd get a nice hotel, hang out a few days, head down to Beale Street say, or take a ride on a riverboat.

The day of, I go to a busy mall near the target. Maybe I'm wearing a particular hat or jacket. I park and go into the mall. Maybe I buy a hat or a jacket. I wear the different hat or the different jacket or maybe I take off the hat or jacket when I exit the mall on the far side. This is all for the camera's benefit. It hardly matters. I have white skin and blue eyes. Nobody ever suspects me of anything. I stroll into the parking lot and pick out a car. I try to find the most common kind of car, Chevy, Ford, stock, nothing fancy, usually white, silver or gray. I have a handy-dandy electronic key that will unlock and start most late-model vehicles. I steal the car—this takes 10-20 seconds. I drive to the location. I walk in, and I meet with the bank officer, whoever. He calls security, and I disarm them. Everyone cooperates—that's company policy. I never take the money from the teller's tills—that's where they keep the dye packs. I drive away slowly—I want them to see the car. I return the car to the mall, as near as possible to where I stole it. The whole thing has taken less than ten minutes and usually the car hasn't even been missed. And if it has, do you know how many people lose their cars in parking lots every day? You've probably done it yourself. I head back to the hotel, have a couple of drinks from the mini-bar, and turn in early. I have a long drive ahead of me tomorrow.

That's pretty much it. You give the fence his 60 and keep your 40. You can do very well on any job that's worth setting up. The problem most guys run into is they like to live high. I've always had simple tastes, never believed a man should be a slave to his passions. All things in moderation. Nothing too much. I think I'm essentially an Epicurean: I believe that the highest good in life is pleasure, i.e, living well, good food, good wine, the best pot, pharmaceutical grade coke, discriminating lovers. But living well doesn't include overindulgence, for on that side lie disaster and death. Ultimately, the highest form of pleasure is the life of the mind.

I invested my money. Paid my taxes like any good citizen. That's how I earned my early retirement. That's how I found my quiet life. And that's why I was so fucking bored.

3

You probably know Austin's reputation as a great music town, but it was actually a haven for all the arts. Sometimes it seemed like every fruit and nut in the great state of Texas lived there, and the swelling influx from both coasts was turning the place into a paradise for hipsters and purgatory for everybody else. The traffic was horrible.

When I retired, I decided to put my energy into the arts. I've always liked the arts, I had the time and money, so why not give it a try?

I went out to some clubs and managed to connect with some like-minded people. Geoff was on vocals and rhythm guitar; I played lead. At this point, I was known as Alex Hardy. I never wanted to have too common a name, nor too distinctive. Skinny Don was on bass and Big Don on drums. We played a lot of covers and a few originals, kind of folk rock I guess you could say, meaning we could rock pretty hard yet play some pretty soulful ballads. Geoff had a nice Gibson jumbo acoustic and played a Telecaster on the rocking numbers. I usually took out my Les Paul and Strat. Sometimes Randy sat in on keys; he was better than all the rest of us put together. We gigged around town every once in a while, or played a wedding or something, and every once in a long while we'd drive down to Corpus or Midland or something for a one-night stand. Truth to tell, if you're a four or five piece band, you lose money on gigs like that. But what the hell—you get to live out your boyhood fantasy of being a rock star. They say you play guitar you get more ass than a toilet seat, and there's some truth in that. I'm certainly not immune to the ego-boost of a getting my rocks off with a hot chick 15 years younger than me, but for some reason, afterwards, I feel lonelier than before.

We were pretty good, not bad. I'm a pretty good musician. I know enough about music to know that I'm good but I'm not that good. We were never going to be the Beatles, we were never going to be the Stones, hell, we were never even going to be Coldplay. But I don't love music any less, maybe more. I just love to play. I become thoroughly alive in the moment each beat hits the air.

Not long after I moved to Austin I enrolled in an art class. We met at a museum in an old mansion by the river. There were a couple of kids in junior high, a couple in their forties, and some little old ladies in their sixties or seventies. I was the only cool person in the room. Then the teacher came in, and she was super hot. It didn't take me many sessions to figure out I have little talent and no patience for painting. I ended up dating the teacher, Jane, for a while. She was good in bed, but strange. She was obsessed with surfaces, but she couldn't or wouldn't go to any depth. I never knew that would matter to me, but it did.

There's a certain centrifugal pull to the Austin arts scene, and a lot of cross-pollination. Through a musician I knew I met a dancer, Elizabeth. Oh my god, what a body. She was tall, six foot even, only an inch shorter than me. I'd never been with a woman that tall; it required a whole new geometry. She was blonde and limber and lithe and strong. At first, I couldn't get enough of her. But inevitably when you sleep with a woman you have to talk to her. You couldn't have a conversation with Elizabeth. Oh, she talked. She talked all the time she was conscious, and sometimes even in her sleep. She leapt and darted from thought to thought like a hummingbird from flower to flower. She made absolutely no sense that I could ascertain. Nor could she listen. She could never make sense of anything I said and got all hurt or mad because she thought I said no when I said yes or vice versa.

Along about then I started making small grants to artists. I helped a songwriter with a few bucks toward recording her first album. I sponsored some needy students to study in Mexico with Jane, and fell in love with San Miguel de Allende. I helped fund a performance for Elizabeth's troupe. I underwrote a publishing project of a poet I was dating—Marguerite—don't ask. She had everything. She was the most gifted and talented, beautiful and miserable person I ever met. I started putting some money behind theatrical productions, and actually saw a small return on my money. That's when I met Charlotte—an actress. I know. I should have known better. She was beautiful. Of course. She was an incredible diva. Of course. She was a drama major, and major drama.

Charlotte was always late because she had to make an entrance. She only lived when all eyes were on her. She went to great lengths to look good, yet if she thought you were admiring her for her looks she got mad. I never could tell what she was thinking or feeling because she was always acting. One of the greatest pleasures of sex, to me, is watching the changes that cross a woman's face when she comes. Charlotte made a lot of noise, but I had the sneaking suspicion she never really came at all.

I put a little money in a short she had the lead in. Well, she had the lead because I put in the money. The thing was about half shot and the money mostly spent when she got into a dispute with the director, walked off the set and refused to work with him ever again. She never really said exactly what the problem was. The director didn't know either. I dumped her.

That's where my head was at when I went out on a shoot as a featured extra, as a lark, as a favor to a friend. The director had no idea why I was even there and I was shunted off to an assistant—and that's when I met Ava. She gave me a quick once-over and said, "Sit at the bar."

I grinned. "What's my motivation?"

She smiled like that wasn't funny and turned to her other tasks.

As I was sitting there waiting, I made up my own motivation—my divorce was final and I was ready to get laid.

I was sitting right next to the principles, a guy in skinny jeans and a plaid shirt, and a cute girl I really couldn't see with him. I had an extraordinarily intimate view of the production. The director had no idea what he was doing. He shot the scene over and over and the poor actors were lost and exhausted. It would have been funny if it weren't so sad.

I kept watching Ava. I didn't know her name yet. She had her hair caught up in a clip and the ends bobbled in a funny way. She wore dark-rimmed glasses low on her nose. She wasn't wearing any make-up. She clearly had a nice rack under that T-shirt, but her bulky utility belt made her ass look kind of fat. I liked the way she took charge. Later I found out she was the assistant director, the person who makes everything happen. I loved watching her work. She moved from technician to technician, lining out their tasks. She handled about five hundred half-assed questions and solved at least that many problems. She moved with confidence and control. She knew what she was doing. She was in the zone.

4

About that time I realized not all of us can be good at a lot of things. I tried giving my time, my talent and my attention to a lot of things, and I wasn't very good at any of them. Sometimes, try as you might, you're only really good at one thing. I came to believe that a person has a duty to pursue with all his or her energy and hopes and dreams and passion that one thing.

I had remained totally incognito since arriving in Austin, but I already knew of a major fence. I contacted somebody I knew, who talked to somebody he knew, and he talked to somebody he knew. The word unerringly reached him. And I heard back the same way.

I scoped out the place long before our meeting. His cover was a compound pawn shop, car wash, tow service, used car lot and junkyard. The rusting hulks sprawled for a half a mile among pecans and live oaks along the riverbank on the far east side of town. Let's call the man Johnson—he looked like Lyndon Johnson, only meaner and uglier. He did a lot of cash business, he was turning over cars and boats and motorcycles, tools and jewelry, all kinds of merchandise every day, he employed a whole bunch of ex-cons, giving him a ready pool of talent, and he was in tight with the cops. The perfect set-up.

A big angle-iron gate fronted the compound. I stepped through the man-gate on the side. A great big black guy blocked the path. I wonder why people automatically think bigger is badder.

He led me into a dark, narrow hallway that he nearly filled. I could have taken him out with one kick behind the knee. The structure seemed to consist of at least three different buildings grafted together. We turned several times and went up and down stairs till we came to a heavy door where he knocked. A low sound came from the other side; he pushed open the door and let me into a low, dark office with a nasty brown carpet on the floor and what looked like the same thing on the walls. The sliding glass door opened onto a concrete balcony overhung by a massive live oak. The smell of mildew was strong.

Johnson pulled out a big, turd-shaped cigar, fired it, let it go out, stuffed it into his cheek and chomped down. He never took it out of his mouth nor spit the whole time I was there.

He made a sound like a laugh. "So you're looking for a job?"

"No, I'm looking for work."

"Same difference."

"No, I'm an independent contractor. I work with you, not for you."

"No need to be so touchy." He grinned around the cigar. "I heard about some of them jobs you did up north. St Louis? Lexington? Somewhere in Ohio, was it?

"Something like that."

"Yeah? Yeah, well, I got something could be something coming up in a few weeks here."

"What's the deal?"

"The usual."

"Yeah?"

We sat there looking at each other.

"I ain't gonna give you the particulars till I know you're in."

"Well, I'm not getting in till I know the particulars."

"Yeah?"

"Yeah. Like where?"

"In the Metroplex."

"Huh?"

He grinned and shook his head. "DFW. The Dallas-Fort Worth area."

"I never work in the same state where I'm living."

"Is that a fact?" He looked at me like I was stupid. "Son, you're in Texas now."

I looked at him like I know where I'm at.

"You're new here. Texas is its own world. We got ever kind of country and ever kind of people there is, black, white, brown, yellow—not too many reds, run them out a long time ago—but we all believe in one thing and that's freedom, firearms and football. We got our own way of doing. Am I making myself clear to you, boy?"

"Not very."

"I don't get into no interstate commerce. All of my business is right here in this great state of ours. Texas is a big place. Texas ain't the South, we ain't the West, we ain't the Mid-West and we sure as hell ain't Mexico, but somehow or another we're all of them. We got a little bit of everthing and everbody—everthing I want and everbody I need."

I weighed my options. I probably could still have backed out at this point. Maybe. But I asked for this meeting. I asked for this job. I asked for this.

Johnson gave me a name, a place, a time.

"Anything should go wrong?" he said. "You contact me. You come to me,

16

I bring you in. Because if anything should go wrong and you don't contact me, you don't come to me? I can only conclude that's because you're trying to cut me out. Now, you don't want me thinking that."

"I'm a businessman. I'm a professional. I perform a highly specialized service. I will be there on the spot to expedite the transaction. I command a very large sum for this service because I take on the greatest share of the risk. Anything should go wrong, I've got my own insurance, and non-disclosure is a given."

"I want a no-compete clause. Long as you work for me, you work only for me."

"That seems reasonable."

5

As I may have said before, robbing a bank is no big deal. Getting away with it is.

Anybody, literally anybody, can walk into a bank and hold it up. You don't even need a gun. It's against company policy to resist a robber, though the sneaky little bastards will slip a dye-pack in on you. So any dumbass can just waltz into a bank and waltz out with a few thousand bucks. That's not a problem. The problem is, most often the very next thing you waltz into is jail.

Some guys (or gals) actually get away with it for a while, but really, that is no way to make a living, and they do get caught.

To get away with a few hundred thousand is an entirely different matter. And getting away from the scene of the crime is just the beginning. Don't forget, you're going to have to find some way to ease that cash back into the economy without drawing the attention of the almighty IRS. Of course, you can blow it on cocaine in a matter of weeks if you want. But then, what's the point?

I made a couple of trips to the Metroplex, as they say. First time, I flew in and stayed at the airport hotel. I rented a car and went to the guitar show in Arlington, and caught a Ranger's game. I picked up a chick from Thailand in the bar and took her back to my room. I wanted to be sure to leave a footprint.

I spent two solid days thoroughly familiarizing myself with Mesquite, the area in question. I examined every approach and exit, every street and alley, every fair sized parking lot, and drew meticulous maps. I spent nothing but cash.

The second time I stayed in downtown Fort Worth and caught an impressionist show at the Kimball. I checked everything out again. I wanted to know those streets like I grew up there.

When the time came, I drove.

The appointment wasn't until three. I packed some fruit, trail mix, a sandwich and a couple of liters of water. I left at eight. I topped off my tank in Georgetown, about 30 miles north, part of the ugly, depressing sprawl that surrounds every American city. I paid cash. I didn't want to leave a paper trail. In retrospect, I wasn't going to be anywhere near Dallas today.

Somewhere north of Temple I pulled off the interstate and found a little dirt road that ran behind a clump of bushes and peed. Let's see them find that DNA. South of Waco I went through a little town where there was a little bank on one side of the highway and a little savings and loan on the other. I thought how funny... Nah, fuck that.

I drove straight on to the mall I had picked out. Man this place was just about the back end of nowhere. I mean, if you had to think of a more squalid, generic, tilt-wall, quiet resignation, you couldn't. It was perfect.

I stole a white Ford, drove to the location, met the guy, showed security the gun, completed the transaction and drove back to the mall in six minutes flat.

Traffic was light, and a half hour later I was in Waxahachie, listening to Tom Petty and cruising on cruise control. I stopped to pee in the bushes again somewhere south of Hillsboro.

I met Johnson's "attorney," a sleazy little dweeb named Virgil something, at a Mexican restaurant on East 7th Johnson probably owned through a front. After a brief chat about the weather, I split, leaving my bag in the booth.

I stopped at the store and went back to my place. I put away the groceries.

I went to my bedroom and dumped the last grocery bag on my bed. I stood there looking at the pile of hundreds. A hundred and fifty thousand bucks. That was stupid. What do I want with a hundred and fifty thousand bucks? That ain't shit. That ain't nothing but trouble.

The goddamn doves were cooing so loud I could hardly think.

6

I was still a little disgusted with myself when I went out that night. I had a pocket full of cash and I intended to throw some around.

The short I was extra in, "Thursday Morning," was showing for the first time, and probably the last, in a little fanboy festival at a soulless multiplex in South Austin. Sure it would be full of geeks and nerds, but I figured there had to be at least some hot women. And I was genuinely curious to see what the movie was all about. I only knew the one scene I was in.

Afterwards, I still only had a vague idea, something to do with on-line role-playing gamers who were a little uncertain about their sexuality. My scene was cool, though. I'm sitting at the bar right next to the leads nursing a beer. Even though I never say anything it's like you can tell what I'm thinking. The looks I give them while they ramble on are pretty funny—I actually got a laugh.

I slipped out of the theater and went looking for where they kept the good-looking women, which I figured was in the bar. They certainly weren't hanging around in the lobby; the festival attendees were a pasty-faced bunch of couch potatoes, as far as I could see, and they dressed the part—hoodies, plaid shirts, canvas sneakers. I saw one girl wearing pajama bottoms and fuzzy slippers carrying a stuffed animal. By virtue of my button-down and blazer I was probably the best dressed guy in the place.

I found the bar under a tent in the parking lot. I stood in line to buy a crappy, overpriced margarita. I spotted someone I knew and was starting his way when I noticed two women at a table smiling at me. When I say smiling, I mean really smiling, these big, open, welcoming smiles, like they knew me or something. This happens pretty often—I get approached by women in bars—so I thought no big deal and moseyed over to their table. They were dressed like this was Hollywood, an Oscar party, instead of a would be, wanna be, never gonna be. The blonde was tall and had big tits and she wasn't afraid to show them off.

"You're such a comedian," she said.

I may have shrugged or arched my eyebrows. Let them do the talking's always a good idea.

"You reminded us of Curly," the brunette said," you know, from the Three Stooges."

"Only better looking," the blonde said.

They laughed. "In the scene where he's trying to eat the clam chowder," the brunette said. They laughed again.

"I don't get the joke."

"I'm sorry, I feel like I know you," said the brunette. "I've been staring at your face for the last month and a half."

They laughed some more. I was beginning to feel, something, off balance, somehow. "Such a nice face," said the blonde, and they both laughed, the brunette covering her mouth with her hand.

"Thanks, I think."

They stood. "We're being rude," the brunette said.

The blonde extended her hand. "I'm Lana," she said, "the producer." She was a real head-turner, a hell of a lot of woman. She was stacked and packed and looked like she could crush a walnut between her thighs.

"I'm Ava," the brunette said as we shook hands. "The editor."

I looked at her closely for the first time. She wasn't as showy as the blonde, but there was something about her, something powerful but shy, something fierce but yielding, like she could be the sexiest woman alive. Her eyes were either brown or green or both, I could never decide. Her hair wasn't really brunette—that was the overall effect—but rather made up of strands of every color known to man, black, brown, red, gold, silver and white. I learned this later when I studied her hair under a magnifying glass while she slept. That's how far gone I was.

"You know, on the, uh…." She tilted her head toward the theater.

Then it hit me. "Guess I'm kind of slow on the uptake."

"No," Lana said, "we should have said something. It's just we've looked at your scene so many times. You really are funny."

"A natural talent," Ava said.

Lana was in her mid-to-late 20s, but Ava, I couldn't tell. She could be 25, she could be 35, she could be 45.

"Probably the best scene in the whole movie," said Lana.

"Yeah, it's pretty lame," Ava said.

"But you're talking about your own movie. Why'd you even make it?"

"I was just helping out a friend," Lana said, "because I didn't want to see him make a complete fool of himself." She shrugged. "Guess I failed."

"I needed the paycheck," said Ava. I studied her. There was just something about her, her eyes, her hair, her voice. I felt like I should know her, like I'd known her all my life and maybe before that. She looked a little like my mother.

I heard myself say, "I feel like I've seen you before." I kind of cringed.

She scrunched up her face like that was the oldest pickup line in the world.

"Like maybe in a dream, or another life." I couldn't stop myself.

"You don't remember?"

I stared. I stared and stared. It was embarrassing. I was missing something.

"I was AD."

I thought about that. Anno Domini?

"Assistant director?" Her smile was fading.

"Oh, yeah, yeah." This was that girl? I groped for words. "But you look so…so…" I sounded like I felt—stupid.

"She cleans up nice," said Lana.

We all had a good laugh. I drained my cup.

"Let's get the hell out of here," I said, "and go somewhere where we can get something decent to drink."

I suggested this upscale bar and grill not far from my house. I knew I could drop several hundred there. If everything went well, maybe a grand. Since my retirement, I was driving a Beamer, gunmetal blue. Looking back, the Toyota was actually a better car, but right then I was glad because I knew I looked good in it. They followed in a nice little red Honda two-seater, Lana at the wheel. We ordered a round of top shelf drinks, single-malt for me, martinis for the ladies. Honestly, gin's gin—I don't see what can be top shelf about a martini, but what the hell, they were expensive. I ordered some sushi and a blue crab appetizer. There went 75 bucks right there.

We talked about the usual for a while. We commented on the food and drinks. Everybody's so into food these days maybe America is waking up from its long, generations long, national nightmare of hasty and tasteless eating. Nah. I'll believe that when pigs fly, or that is, when the mainstream American flies. Nice to know that if you're physically fit you're out of the mainstream, since two-thirds of our fellow citizens are overweight or obese, to say nothing of the morbidly obese. Well, these girls were definitely not in the mainstream.

Most people find me friendly, sociable, a good conversationalist—an extrovert, to be brief, when the truth is the exact opposite. People think I'm a good talker because I'm a good listener. People just naturally like to open up to me because I ask them questions about themselves, and surprise, people like to talk about themselves. Many times I've talked at length with someone, usually a woman, and come away knowing everything about her, her life history, her relationship status and the status of all her past relationships, sexual preferences, life and career hopes, fears, aspirations, and in the process have revealed little to nothing about myself. After a catharsis like that, some people are hard to get rid of.

Lana had a Harvard MBA and was living at home—her dad was a lawyer —trying to get her start as a producer. She was interning with a semi-big-name director who was, according to her, a douche, and looking around for her next project now that she'd wrapped "Thursday Morning."

"By the way, what does the title have to do with anything?"

"Nothing. It's when he wrote the script, what there was of it."

"Really?"

"I tried to talk him out of it."

Ava was a film school graduate from UCLA who was trying to make a go of it on her skills—and she had serious skills. She could shoot, light, record, do literally anything on a set including craft service (the food). She laughed. But she really wanted to direct.

"You know, you two have just about the perfect names for film."

They laughed and traded glances like it was an inside joke.

After the first drink the girls went to the restroom. This was going well. My place was literally right around the corner.

When they came back I had replacements on the table. Ava slid into the booth but Lana remained standing.

"Oh, no," she said, "I can't. I've got to drive all the way out to the lake, and tomorrow's an early day." After a fake little hug, she split.

Ava and I ordered entrees. In this place, burgers were like 25 bucks. My sea bass was 70-something, and her scallops over 50. I guess she was trying to economize, not to look too greedy. I bought a 200-dollar bottle of wine— didn't want to overdo it.

We sat there for three solid hours. She drank the last martini, slowly, not to let it go to waste, she said. I ordered another Scotch. She was the easiest person to talk to I had ever met. For once, it was like I didn't have to do all the work. I was actually enjoying myself.

She asked me about my mom and dad. God, it had been so long since I had even thought of them. I told her how lonely I felt, growing up. I don't think I even realized that until that very moment. I told her about the time I first understood my true power, when I took the gun from Bennett.

"You hit him?" she said.

"I was just a kid back then. I would never do that today. Violence is stupid. I abhor violence. But sometimes, I guess, some people just don't understand anything else."

"So where did you go to school?"

"Florida State." I can't believe I told her the truth.

"What was your major?"

I told her that too.

"Aren't psychology majors crazy?"

"Yeah, as everyone's always reminding us."

"Sorry."

"Not a new joke."

She smiled—magic.

The waiter let us know the place was closing. The bill was a little over 600 bucks. I laid down eight. She watched me throw those bills on the table like any woman would. I just about had this.

We went to the car. "I don't live far," she said.

I drove cautiously. I didn't want to run afoul of the law at a time like this. She lived in a townhouse. I walked her to the door. I took her in my arms. She smelled so nice. I leaned in to kiss her. She turned her head at the last second and I pecked her on the cheek.

"I have an early call," she said. "I enjoyed our chat, but I'm going to regret that last martini."

She smiled sweetly and closed the door behind her. I stood there for a minute or two. I couldn't believe it.

Driving home, I couldn't get her off my mind. I spent 800 bucks. I mean, what a bitch. No. I couldn't think of her like that—it hurt too much. I could still smell her. I thought about everything we had said. I wanted her so bad I thought I would bust wide open.

I got home and went into my empty bedroom. I opened the dresser draw and stood there looking at the cash—a hundred and fifty thousand bucks, minus dinner.

7

I slept badly. The next day I felt about half hung over. I had acted like an asshole, throwing money around as if a woman of her intelligence and sensitivity would tumble over a few hundred bucks. On the other hand, what woman wouldn't be interested when I flashed that kind of cash, unless I was some kind of asshole and she was just taking advantage of me?

I ate a little breakfast, checked my investments and read a few articles on line. I paced around the house not knowing what to do with myself. I sat outside for a while and watched the cats sleep. I drove down to Town Lake and jogged on the hike and bike trail, then went swimming at Deep Eddy. After a shower and a nap I felt a little better. I picked up my Les Paul and jammed out for a while cranked up through this insane overdrive pedal into my boutique amp. This rig is awesome. Electric guitar—there's nothing else that makes you feel so powerful. A gun makes you feel powerful, yeah. But strap on that guitar and you've got a fleet of helicopter gunships and you're on a mission from god raining hell and death from above, shock and awe, baby. I kept fucking up and forgetting what I was doing. When you're playing music, you can't think. If you think, you get distracted, and you fuck up. I kept getting distracted.

I wanted to call her. But that was stupid because I never call them, they always call me. The "rules" say you're supposed to wait three days after meeting her before calling a woman and ask her out by Wednesday for Saturday. What bullshit. Do that, and no woman would ever respect you. I made it a point never to ask for a woman's number. She ought to have sense enough to see she needs to make her move before someone cuts in on her action. But I wanted to call her and I didn't have her number.

I started to look for Ava on Facebook but I couldn't remember her last name. I couldn't remember if she told me. There was no page for the movie. I couldn't remember Lana's last name either, if I ever heard. If that was her name. Lana and Ava. What the hell? No wonder they laughed. They were laughing at me.

The one thing I knew was where she lived. That was something. That was a lot. I could just get in the car and… No. I couldn't do that. She'd recognize my car. She'd think I was stalking her. She'd know I was interested and… No. In every relationship one person loves the other more, and the person who loves the least has the most power. I've always made sure I was the one with the power.

She didn't live far. Maybe I could go by on my bicycle just to see what I could see and not be seen. No. How pathetic.

I looked at the movies on cable and pay-per-view and on-line services, and everything looked like crap. I started streaming one almost at random. I couldn't even follow the stupid, pathetic plot because it was so stupid and pathetic. I paced around the house and said, no way, I'm not the guy that paces around the house.

I put on my shorts and helmet, got on my bike and started pedaling. A deep sense of calm settles over me very quickly when I get on the bicycle. It's all about focus and control. You don't have to think but just do. I drove to her house. I slowed down and pedaled slowly by. Didn't look like anyone was home. I turned around at the end of the block and pedaled past again. This was stupid. What had I hoped to learn? I stood up and rode that machine like I was climbing Mont Ventoux in the Tour de France. I burned as hard as I could as fast as I could as long as I could. I got home after dark.

I took another shower. I ate some granola. I went to bed with a book and read far into the night.

8

I stayed in. I went out. When I stayed in I wished I was going out and when I went out I wished I had stayed at home. I couldn't concentrate on music and felt disgusted with my playing. I wandered around the yard looking for something to weed or trim. There was nothing. I couldn't even read. Reading has always been my refuge, my redoubt. I searched and searched and could find nothing on my shelves, nor in the bookstore.

I didn't feel like eating but you have to eat. I went to the super new upscale grocery story. It was full of beautiful women. I saw this brunette, kind of big and small at the same time, if you know what I mean, kind of round and skinny, curvy and sporty and I was about to speak when she turned around and it wasn't her.

I was just bored. I needed something to do. I needed something to put my mind to so I'd have something else to think about. I contacted Virgil on a pre-paid phone and met him at the restaurant.

I took a job in San Antonio—close enough to work from home. I drove down for a Spurs game. The interstate was nightmarish, some sort of futuristic death race. At the game, I was so bored I felt like I was in church. I left before halftime. Why did I even bother?

I drove through idiotic traffic to the northwest suburbs. San Antonio is ringed by miles and miles of particularly ugly sprawl. I found the place, in one of those satellite downtown areas of glass-plated high-rise offices. I scoped it out from the parking lot across the street in front of a mega-grocery and miles long stretch of strip malls, one of those constricted, Californicated spaces. There was a lot of activity, lots of traffic and people coming and going. I went into the store and bought a bottle of water so I was a customer. I went back to my car. I drank my water. I looked out of place here, I decided. I drove around looking for a more upscale mall or something. I didn't like the look of anything. I drove back toward town. I drove about ten miles before I found anything I could use. I went in and ate at an overpriced Mexican restaurant where everything was so generic I would have done better at a chain. I didn't like this town. I went home on 281, which is west of the interstate and a little more scenic, trying to avoid the traffic. I shouldn't have bothered. What a mess.

I was never so glad to get home. I opened a beer and kicked back in my favorite chair. I took a sip, then another. I sat there staring at the wall. I went outside and had another beer. It was getting near dark. I watched the neighborhood cats do their thing. They have their own social system all to themselves.

An interminable two days later I was back in San Antonio. I went straight to the mall and jacked the first likely looking car I saw, a white Toyota Camry, ten years old but in good shape. Perfect. I drove to the location and entered the parking garage. I had to punch the button to get a ticket, and I saw the camera looking right at me. It's amazing what a little make-up can do to alter a person's appearance, a bit of definition on the cheekbones, glasses with heavy dark frames, a high quality mustache. I was wearing a bow tie, which made me look kind of nerdy, I thought.

I went up the elevator, found the right firm, entered and asked for the person. I had an appointment. I waited in the lobby. I was escorted back by security. I entered the office, flashed my piece and disarmed the guard. The contact bagged the cash and I split, just like that. I ran down the stairs, got in the car, paid the attendant and rolled onto the street.

I got back on the freeway and headed for the other location. Traffic was heavy; this was taking longer than I liked. I pulled off my exit. On this side of the mall were a couple of cop cars with their lights flashing. I kept going past the mall and pulled into the parking lot on the other side. I walked through the mall and exited where the cops were talking to a distraught old man.

"It was stolen, I'm telling you," he said.

"Are you sure you didn't just forget where you parked it?" said the beefy blonde cop.

I walked to my Beamer and cruised out of there. That was too close.

I drove home. I was already bored. I took my money and dumped it in the drawer. I dropped the rest with Virgil and got another job, in Beaumont.

Way on the other side of Houston, almost to the Louisiana line, Beaumont is a nasty little refinery town with a busy port and a lot of money. You couldn't pay me to live there. I drove around checking out the scene in what passes for the downtown area. I felt conspicuous. I got out of there pretty quick and continued east all the way to New Orleans, another four or five hours but the closest city with any cool. I stayed in a nice hotel near the Quarter, ate good seafood, got drunk, got laid and spent the next day lying around the hotel pool bored out of my skull. I got up about five the next morning and left before it was light. I drove to Beaumont and parked on a side street around the corner from the oil bank. It took a long minute to walk there. I felt visible and vulnerable on the empty sidewalk. I went inside and took care of business. One of the security guards tried to give me some shit but the contact person told him to shut up and follow company policy. I tried not to run to the car. I hopped in, drove around two corners and was back on the interstate within a minute. I didn't like doing it that way, but it was quick.

I was so fucking bored on the drive home. Traffic was really slow all the way through Houston. I wanted to jump right out the sunroof.

I finally got home, poured a shot and sat back in my chair. I turned on the TV. There was nothing I wanted to watch.

I went to bed and woke up in the middle of the night thinking of her.

9

I stood there looking at the money—close to half a million dollars—which filled the double-deep bottom drawer of my antique dresser. I was forming a plan.

I took a shower and dressed carefully in the kind of thing I'd wear on stage with my band—Geoff's band, actually, I just played guitar—a pair of jeans so worn they were hardly blue anymore and one knee showing through, ostrich-skin cowboy boots and a snap-button western shirt—no hat. I could barely stand to wear a hat unless as part of a disguise, they're so fussy and fuddy-duddy and you never know what to do with them when you're indoors, and trust me, chicks don't dig guys in hats. I gargled before I went out, and took a deep breath.

I pulled up openly in front of her house. I walked proudly and deliberately to her front door and knocked. I stood there. I didn't hear anything. I waited another few seconds and knocked louder. Nothing. I looked around. A couple of cats were watching me from across the street. I pushed the doorbell, as I should have in the first place. Still nothing. I stood there feeling stupid. I walked quickly to the car and drove away.

This was pathetic. I was pathetic. What was I thinking, that I'd just drive up there, give her the proposition and fall into bed?

I pulled into the parking lot of the local downscale grocery. I sat there a few seconds getting myself under control. Nobody had seen me, except the cats.

I went in to get a 12-pack. I felt one coming on. I went straight to the beer aisle. And right there, reading the label on a bottle of cheap wine, there she was.

"Oh, hi," I said, before I could think.

She turned and smiled a great big genuine smile. "Oh, hi!"

"You're looking good." And so she was, in a tight tank-top and yoga pants.

She looked me over in my stagey get-up and smiled even bigger. "Wow, you, uh, too."

"I have a gig," I said, and immediately regretted it. "Uh how's it going? How's show business."

She sagged. "Oh, okay. Let's see, since I met you, I've been on three jobs. Last two weeks I was in Marfa on a stupid horror movie that will never go anywhere."

She kept turning the bottle in her hands. Her fingers were long, her wrists were delicate, her arms were strong. I looked her in the eye. I must have had lovesick whipped puppy written all over me.

"I kept thinking I'd see you again," she said, "like at another event or something."

"I wanted to call you," I said, "but I guess I got so caught up in the moment I forgot to ask for your number."

She was just so pert and pretty and expectant. Her eyes were dilated and moist. "Uh, do you have time to talk?" I said. "Get a cup of coffee or a glass of wine?"

She looked annoyed. "I'd love to, but I've got something in the oven at home. I just dashed over here for..." I could see her making a decision. "Look," she said, "you were so nice the other day and I could never afford anything like that, but why don't you come over, I mean if you have time, and join me for dinner?"

I must have stared.

"Do you like enchiladas? You'll love my enchiladas."

I took the bottle from her and we went to the checkout. We waited there calmly like any couple. I basked in her glow. I walked her to her car, a Prius showing its age, and gave her a little hug. I could feel how firm and full her breasts were. I went to my car and followed her home. We parked in back and entered through a lovely little garden area with orchids in bloom.

"Orchids?" I said. "My mother grew orchids. How do they survive the winter here?"

"I have to bring them inside," she said.

The interior smelled delicious. The look was minimalistic, kind of stylized. We went into the kitchen. She took a corkscrew from a drawer and got two glasses while I opened the wine.

We went into the living room and sat down on the couch.

"Uh, I wanted to talk to you about, uh..." I started.

She set her glass on the coffee table and moved a little closer. I set down my glass. She touched my hand. I took her in my arms and kissed her like my life depended on it.

In five minutes her yoga pants were on the coffee table, her tank top was in the hallway and her panties were lost somewhere in the tangle of covers we kicked off the bed.

I knew right away she was the one. All my life I've looked for a woman who could, at least while we were making love, make me forget all other women. She was it.

I'm not the kind to kiss and tell. I don't want to talk about her in that way. But I had never experienced anything like that before. She was a real take-charge kind of gal. She knew what she liked and what she liked she really, really liked and she wasn't afraid to show me. Specifically, I had never, or seldom, been satisfied with the quality of oral sex most women deign to deliver. I mean, I like oral sex, giving and getting. I've never yet met a woman who didn't like getting, but as for being really enthusiastic and skillful at giving, well, that's a rarity. But this girl, this Ava, she knew how to get the job done, and she really seemed to enjoy herself. I know some of you ladies don't want to think it's all that important, but it is.

After about an hour that felt like about two minutes—no, like an eternity, like we existed outside of time—we were lying there tangled in each other when there was a sudden loud buzz and I kind of jumped. She held me. "The enchiladas are ready," she said. I sat up but she pulled me down. "They'll stay warm," she said.

After we cooled off, she put on her robe and went to the kitchen. I got dressed and followed. The wine was barely acceptable, but the enchiladas were excellent.

"Mmm, what is this?" I asked.

"Artichoke," she said proudly. I took another bite—it was creamy and nutty and buttery and just a little bitter. "I adapted my mom's recipe for chicken enchiladas," she said.

"Amazing," I said.

Afterwards we went back to the couch. I took her in my arms and snuggled her. "There's nowhere I'd rather be and no one I'd rather be with," I told her.

"Don't you have a gig?"

"I had one."

She looked at me funny.

"No, Ava, I want to be completely truthful with you."

"You're not in a band?"

"No. I mean, I am in a band, but..." I couldn't lie to her. I didn't want this to start with a lie. "Earlier today, before we met, you know, I came by here." She was staring at me now. "I wanted to see you, to talk to you, and......"

She smiled. "You dressed like that?"

"I wanted you to notice me."

She kissed me. "You're so cute," she said.

Opening up to her actually felt good. "You're all I've thought about," I said. "I've been going out of my mind thinking about you."

"Why didn't you just come by?"

"I didn't want you to think I was stalking you," I said, which was true.

"Don't be silly." She kissed me again. "You better not forget to ask for my number again," she said.

We kissed some more.

"I have an early call," she said.

I got her number and left.

10

I waited all day till what I thought would be after work to call her and went straight to voicemail. I didn't leave a message. I mean, who leaves messages? She'd see I called and… No. Her phone wouldn't know me. I texted her: "Alex here. Call me."

She called late. There was a lot of talking and laughing in the background. "Hey, how's it going," I said.

"It's a wrap," she said. "What a day. These people are insane."

Somebody with a British accent said, "Love you too, baby!"

"I hope I never see you again," she yelled.

"What?"

"Not you."

"Oh. Where are you?"

"Just leaving the set." I could hear her get in her car and close the door.

"I was hoping to see you."

"Me too, but we've run so late and…"

"What about tomorrow?"

"I'm leaving for Louisiana." I heard her start her car.

"For how long?"

"I'll be there five days, then I turn around and go to New Mexico."

"Wow."

"Yeah, so I'm out for a couple of weeks."

"Oh."

"Alex, look, I, uh, I really feel something for you, okay? But, well, it seems like all I ever do is work."

"Yeah."

"You know how it is."

"Yeah."

I waited for her to say something. Maybe she was waiting for me.

"Maybe I can come out and visit you in one of those places."

"No, I don't think so. The whole cast and crew, we live like right on top of each other, you know, like it's a dorm or summer camp or something. No, I don't think so."

"Well, I'll call you."

"Okay, but I can't take calls when we're shooting and, you know, talking on the telephone, it's tough, you know?"

"Yeah."

"How about I'll call you?"

"Yeah. Okay."

I waited. She waited.

"Okay, well, good night," I said.

"Bye," she said.

The next two weeks I hung in there somehow. I didn't mind waiting so much, because the uncertainty was gone—mostly. I jogged or biked and swam every day. I would be tanned and rested when she got home. I played guitar for at least an hour a day, and rehearsed with the band a couple of times. I caught up on some of the new releases in the theaters and read half a dozen books. I ate well and drank in moderation. I didn't get drunk. I didn't feel the need.

She called a couple of times and we talked briefly. She was working 12- and 15-hour days, and she was tired. I told her she would have to take a few days off when she got done with this gig, and she said she would. She was right about the telephone. Talking on the phone is just never very satisfying. Somehow it leaves me feeling lonelier than ever.

And then she was home. She needed some time to decompress, she said. She had been working so closely with so many people for so long, she just needed some alone time. I said I understood. The next day I picked her up about two and we went to Deep Eddy. I swam a mile and a half while she napped in the shade of the big pecan. When I lay down beside her I sprinkled some of that cold spring water on her and she yelped. We had a laugh. She lay there on her stomach, all curves. I lay back and let the heat soak into my chilled body. She moved her hand an inch to touch mine. In that moment, I felt as good as I ever had.

By the time I had air dried, I was ready to go back in. She still hadn't been in. "Come on, baby," I said, "you'll love it." She gave me some kind of a look when I said "baby."

We jumped in the deep end. Going from the Texas heat to the 69-degree water is a shock to the system. "Wow, it's cold," she said, like everybody who goes in the water at Deep Eddy for the first time.

"Barton Springs is even colder," I said, "only a couple of degrees but you feel it."

"This is cold enough," she said.

"How long have you lived in Austin?"

"A couple of years," she said, "but I'm hardly ever here. What about you?"

"About the same," I said, "but since I retired I have time to see everything and do everything."

"Must be nice."

"Some days."

We went back to her place. She showered and changed. I got a drink of water and peeked in her refrigerator. Very little to see there. I looked over the books on her shelf and saw some old friends, Hawthorne and Poe, Pound and Plath, Freud and Jung. She had a few classics like Chinatown and The Big Sleep on DVD, along with a whole bunch of really crappy-looking movies with zombies, monsters, ghosts, serial killers, killer clowns, teenage misfits, post-apocalyptic cannibals, etc., etc., etc. These must be the movies she worked on.

She came into the living room just then, looking so fresh and delicious in her little dress. "Oh god," she said, "don't look at those."

"Sorry," I said.

We went to my place. "I like it," she said. "Mid-century modern. These hardwood floors? Nice."

"Yeah, you can't even buy wood like that any more," I said. "All the trees that were big enough have been cut down."

I built a fire and put two ears of corn, an onion and some peppers on the smoker. I let that sit while we had a nice chilled pinot grigio. We chatted and enjoyed our wine like any other couple. After the mesquite burned down to hot coals, I grilled a beautiful, inch-thick rib eye. The steak was fabulous, if I say so myself, but the real piece de resistance was the red bell pepper, which was so sweet it tasted like candy.

I was smelling pretty ripe by then, so I jumped in the shower. Gave her a chance to peek in my icebox. I came out smelling like shampoo and soap instead of smoke and meat. I slipped into some gym shorts and a t-shirt and joined her on the couch where she was looking through Man and His Symbols. She set it aside.

"What a great book," she said.

"And a great mind," I said.

"A little nutty," she said.

"Yeah," I said, "a little."

I took her in my arms and gave her a tender little kiss. She smiled sleepily. I took her to bed. I hung up her dress and gave her one of my t-shirts. I went to turn out the lights and lock up and pee. When I got back to my room, she was fast asleep. I stood there beside the bed counting her breaths for a while before creeping in beside her. I held her and cuddled her and drank in her scent. I felt so good. I felt so happy, contented and satisfied and eager and excited all at the same time. There must be a name for this kind of happiness, but I didn't know it. One thing I did know—I wanted to keep this feeling.

I woke in the night to pee but she never stirred. I lay there a long time listening to her heart, breathing in unison.

We woke at first light and made sweet love. We had breakfast at the neighborhood tacqueria and went back to her place. I sat on the couch while she roamed around the room.

"What next?" I said.

She plopped down in an overstuffed chair. "Another stupid piece of shit. Shooting starts Monday."

"Here in town?"

"Yeah."

"You're AD?"

"Yeah." She sank into the chair. "At least I'm busy."

"You're in demand."

"Yeah." She seemed to sink deeper.

"What's the movie about?"

"More stupid shit. Zombies." She stood up and looked out the window. "You go to school, you dream of making great movies that will change people's lives, and you end up with zombies. I mean, who gives a shit about zombies? Why is everybody so obsessed with zombies?"

"I've thought about that," I said. "I think it's because everybody lives such dead lives. We go to our dead jobs, we come home to our dead relationships, we eat our dead food, we go out for dead entertainment. You ever watch sports? Maybe the players are having fun, but you're just sitting there, bored out of your mind."

She was looking at me. "That's good," she said.

"That would be my zombie movie," I said. "They're all dead from sheer boredom."

She laughed.

"So what would you do," I said, "if you could do anything you wanted to, you know, direct?"

She lit up. "I want to make movies that are so real you think they're real." She started pacing. "I want to make movies that are real, the realest movies that have ever been made."

"How do you mean?"

"I mean movies that are so real you feel like you're actually having the experience." She perched on the edge of the chair. "I mean, Hollywood is so fake. I mean, I love those old studio movies that are so romantic and larger than life. If we're talking about The Wizard of Oz or Singing in the Rain, who cares if they're fake? That's the magic of movies, that they can take you to that place and you're right there singing along with "Ding Dong the Witch is Dead."

I laughed.

"But I love the transparency of Sidney Lumet, you know? It's like the camera's not even there. But most of the time, you know, movies are just fake. I mean, who could be afraid of zombies, you know? Zombies don't even exist."

"I know."

"If I wanted to make a scary movie, I'd make something that would scare your pants off."

"You don't have to do that."

She shook her head. It was a bad joke. "Scary movies sell."

"Yeah?"

"I want to make a scary movie, but I want to make a movie that is so real it really scares the shit out of you. Know what I mean? Really makes you think about some scary shit that's really real." She was pacing again.

"Like what?"

"Like crime."

"Hmm?"

"Like crime. Crime is real. Your chances of getting caught up in the zombie apocalypse are exactly zero. Your chances of getting caught up in a crime? Well, that depends, doesn't it?"

She looked at me significantly. I tried to stay cool.

"What do you mean?"

"I mean, people get involved in crimes every day. They plan it or do it on the spur of the moment, or they're the victims. I once read that every man in America would rob a bank, if he thought he could get away with it. I don't know about the women. But I would."

"You would what?"

"I would without a doubt rob a bank if one, I could get away with it, and two, I could make enough money."

I kind of smiled at her I guess. "How much is enough?"

"I don't know," she said, "maybe a few hundred thousand, you know, half a million, what the hell, make it a million."

"How many robberies do you think you'd have to commit to make that kind of money?"

"I don't know. If I got away with it, what difference would it make?"

"Good point."

"Anyway, I don't want to do any of these indie clichés. I want to do a caper."

"A what?"

"A caper. You know, a crime movie where you follow the planning and execution of the crime and the getaway or they get caught or whatever. I want to make the crime so real that you feel like you actually committed it."

"How much would it cost?"

"Not much. It's pathetic what a little bit of money stands between so many filmmakers and their dreams. But I have to make a living and that takes up all my time—what you love becomes a trap. And trying to raise the money and all that, it's just impossible." She shook her head.

"If you tell yourself it's impossible, it is."

"Spare me."

"How about if I help?"

"Hmm?"

"How about if I finance it, uh, help finance it?"

"You could do that?" She stopped pacing. "You would do that? I mean, I figure you have money, but…"

"I would love to help. I've been sitting here thinking how into all this you are, and how I'd love to help, but…"

She looked at me expectantly.

"I have an ulterior motive," I said. "I want to keep you here, in town, with me. But I don't want you to think that I think I could, you know, that you would, you know, for money…"

"Yeah," she said.

"I don't want to, you know, I'm not trying to…"

"Yeah. It might be kind of awkward."

"But it doesn't have to be," I said. "We can, you know, keep it informal."

"What do you mean?"

"I mean, we can just rock along, I can supply the money when needed, we don't have to draw up any formal contracts or anything like that, you know, we can just kind of do it. Whatever else happens, we can figure out later."

She studied me. "How much are we talking about?"

"How much do you need?"

11

I wanted her to bail on the zombie project but she said she couldn't. "This is a small world," she said. "I'll have to work with these people again."

So that was another two weeks, including weekends, of 12-hour days—for her. I tried to be patient—not my strong suit. Look, I'm a horny guy. I wasn't used to going without, and I didn't want to get used to it. But something in the way I felt for her made me not want anyone else. What made it worse was it was her choice to spurn my offer. Or rather, postpone accepting. It amounted to almost the same thing.

I sought refuge in my usual expedients. I worked out three hours a day, getting madder all the time. I tried to read but couldn't concentrate. The guitars sat on their stands. I dug out a big patch of cactus not because it needed doing but because I needed to work and sweat till I was bloody.

I took a little job in Sugarland, a suburb of Houston. Everyone in the place was on the hypertension and diabetes diet.

The security guy was morbidly obese. Looked like his knees had just about given out on him. We went to the office of my contact. He was at least 50 pounds overweight. I flashed my piece, a really sweet, antique Colt .32 automatic, like Al Capone carried. Why does everyone think bigger is better? If you can hit what you're shooting at, if you can place that little lump of lead right where you want to, what's the point? The guard looked at me like I was a loser. He put his hand on the butt of his big .357. "I ain't givin' up my gun to a punk like you," he said.

The contact said, "Don't!"

I mean, I had my gun on him. He was supposed to do what I said, right? It's funny. I wanted to shoot him so bad. What an idiot! And he thought I was the punk. I really, really, really wanted to let him have it, right then, right there. And that, right there, is what will put you in prison, or worse—the tiniest slip of self-control. It took every ounce of psychological strength at my command to hold myself in check.

He must have realized. He eased the heavy revolver out of the holster and handed it to me. It was all I could do not to slap him in the face with it.

The contact bagged the cash and I split. I dropped the guard's gun in a garbage can in the parking garage. My hand was shaking, I was still so hot. I got back to my car and headed home. The whole job had only taken six minutes.

As I drove through the serene countryside, I thought about how close I came. "You can't let it get to you like that," I said.

I met Virgil at a different Mexican restaurant. Austin probably had five thousand Mexican restaurants. Who knows how many were fronting for Johnson, or someone like him?

It was only about 2:30 when I got home. I put the money in the drawer— about $30,000. What a joke. On interest alone I probably make that in a month.

12

I tried to put the whole situation in the best possible light. She was staying true to her word and loyal to her friends. That should be a good thing, right? If she was loyal to them, she'd be loyal to me, right?

We went out for dinner the day after she finished her zombie gig. I took her to a quiet little bistro. The cuisine was haute—a fusion of Chinese, Japanese, French, a little of everything. I had the salmon. She had eel. I ordered a nice dry Riesling.

Back at her place, we settled on her couch with an indifferent Chardonnay. I was ready to talk business. I took a small stack of hundreds out of my bag and put it on the coffee table.

"This will get you started," I said.

"What's that?" she said.

"Ten thousand dollars," I said.

"What for?" she said.

"For you," I said. "For your movie."

"I don't have a movie yet. I don't have a script. I don't have a budget."

"Yeah, but you're not going to get one unless you put the time in, right? This is your salary. What do you think, a couple of months?"

"What?"

"Five thousand a month, is that about right?"

She shook her head.

"Not enough?"

"That's a lot."

"What do you mean?"

She stared at me.

"I'm just guessing, but you're in the film industry, you work so much…"

"I've never made anything close to that."

"What?"

"I make around three thousand a month, maybe less."

"How can you live in Austin on thirty thousand a year."

"I manage."

"Well, now you don't have to live like that."

"Like what? Something wrong with the way I live?"

"I didn't mean that."

"I think I do all right. I love my life."

"Of course. But, well, well, you decide how much you need."

"I decide how much of your money I take."

I didn't know what to say. It had never occurred to me that anyone would hesitate to take my money.

I said, "The thing is, I don't give a shit. This ain't shit to me. I'm just trying to help out a friend."

I admit I was miffed. She compressed her lips. "Okay fine," she said.

"What then?"

"You're right," she said. "What the hell."

"Just let me know when you need more."

"One more thing," she said. "Why did you bring it, you know, in cash?"

"This is just extra money I had laying around."

"Really? How come?"

"Look, I play poker with some big spenders who don't know how to play poker. They don't give a shit. So I bring home all this cash. I don't want to report it, because my tax situation means it would end up costing me money. I'd have to pay more in taxes than I won." I really, really hated telling her that. I really, really wanted to trust her completely, but I couldn't trust her that much. "I can't just throw it away."

She looked at me like she knew.

"Really," I said. I felt like a heel.

"Really?"

I couldn't stand it. I loved her too much. "No, baby, I can't lie to you," I said. "Actually, I got it the same way I got all my money."

She was waiting and watching. I felt myself trembling on the edge of an abyss.

"I stole it."

13

She laughed. "You stole it."

I didn't like the tone of her voice.

"Why do you find it so hard just to tell the truth?" she said.

"I'm not lying."

"Okay, where'd you steal it?"

"I don't want to get into particulars," I said. "Lots of places."

"Who'd you steal it from?"

"Nobody that couldn't afford it." I knew that sounded lame. "Nobody that didn't want me to. It's all in the business plan. There's always someone inside that wants the job done. It's all prearranged. The fix is in."

She looked at me from a million miles away.

"This is just another cog in the great American economic machine," I said. "Just the lubricant, really. The system is like clogged with cash, and someone's got to clear out the drains. Then there are the big insurance companies—they need something to do besides cheat people out of their money."

She was smiling a funny little superior smile.

"I don't have to justify myself to you," I said.

"When's your next job?" she said.

"I'm retired."

"Then where'd you get this?"

"I don't have anything lined up right now."

"I want to go along."

"What?"

"I want to go with you on a job."

"That's not going to happen."

"Why not?"

"There's no way. Forget about it."

"I want to know what it's like."

"It's pretty boring, actually."

"I want to film it."

I laughed.

"I'm serious," she said. "I'll make you a star."

"Do you have any idea how insane that is?"

She just kept looking at me. I wasn't going to say another word.

"Look," she said, "if I'm going to make a realistic crime movie I'm going to have to see for myself what a real crime is really like. Right?"

"There's nothing to see."

"Maybe not for you."

"I can't show my face in something like that."

"You can wear a mask."

"I can't wear a mask. I have to go in like any other business person."

'You can wear make-up."

"I already do. Not good enough."

"A good make-up artist can totally change your appearance."

"We can't bring along a make-up artist!"

"Just a minute," she said. She went to her room and came back with a tiny little camera. "You can wear this on your lapel," she said, "and record the whole thing."

"This is stupid," I said.

14

I picked up a job in Burleson, one of the two hundred and something so-called communities that make up the Metroplex. I dressed in black boots and new jeans, a white shirt, black string tie and black jacket. Ava died my hair several shades darker than normal and added some gray at the temples, darkened my eyebrows and gave me a full, dark mustache. I really looked the part.

She was fascinated with the gun. "Think you'll have to shoot anyone?" she said.

"Never," I said. "It's more of a symbol than anything."

She rigged the camera to a crossed-Texas-and-Mexico-flags lapel pin so it was virtually indistinguishable.

We left early and cruised smoothly up the interstate. We ate breakfast in Waco, not that I wanted to but she had to pee, of course, and one thing led to another. I paid cash, so no harm no foul.

She was chattering away like she never does and I was trying to ignore her. She took a good long look at me. I met her eye, and she shut up.

I drove on past Burleson and into Fort Worth before I found a nice enough place near the university to leave the Beamer. I walked Ava into the mall and stopped in front of the first shoe store we came to like we were window-shopping.

"This is where I leave you," I said.

"What do you mean?"

"You'll wait here till I get back."

"No way. I'm going with you."

"No. This is when the dangerous stuff begins."

"But you promised!"

"Hush," I said.

She lowered her voice. "But I've got to be there. I've got to see it, to feel it, to know it."

"That's why I'm wearing this."

"It's not the same."

"It'll have to do."

She was steamed, I could tell. But what could she do? I gave her a couple hundred bucks. "Buy yourself something nice."

I went outside and jacked the first likely looking thing I saw, a white

Chevy pickup about five years old. There must have been 20 of them in the parking lot.

The drive to the location was longer than I liked. On the way I was getting more and more nervous. What I was doing was, frankly, stupid. Not only was I collecting state's evidence on myself, but if Johnson ever found out there was no prison that could protect me. Well, he would never find out. I for sure wouldn't tell him. She was the only other person who would ever know, and she wouldn't tell. She didn't even know Johnson. How could she?

I pulled into the parking lot of the low-rise office building. I sat there for a minute breathing deeply. I debated forgetting to turn on the camera, but the thought of her disappointment, her anger, her resentment, constrained me. She already knew too much. What would she do if she were angry enough?

"No one will ever know," I said.

I strode purposefully into the lobby. I gave the guy at the desk the name of my contact. He called and the guy came out and led me to his office. He called security, per routine. He needed someone to witness the transaction. The guard was a young, gung-ho type, probably ex-military, probably only kind of job a dumb son of a bitch like him could get. I showed him the .32. He got a wild look in his eye and went for his black nine. I slapped him on the wrist with the barrel of my piece and he dropped his. In almost the same motion I swatted him on the bridge of the nose. He clapped his hand to his face and sank to his knees with the blood running down. He bent over and bled all over the carpet. I picked up his gun and leveled it. I could hear a voice in my head screaming no. It was like I was a different person. I looked at the contact. "No," he said. "Please. No one's supposed to get hurt."

He knew immediately what he'd done. His eyes went wide and his mouth hung open—about the funniest thing you've ever seen. The guard looked up at him. Blood was smeared all over his face and running down his shirt. He looked like he'd been drinking blood. Understanding slowly dawned in his eyes.

"You're about as dumb as he is," I told him. I took the money and walked out. The guard at the desk in the lobby was picking up the phone when I came out. I showed him the gun and he put it down. I ran to the truck and hauled ass out of there. I realized I still had the guard's pistol in my hand. I pulled off on a side street and threw it out the window into a vacant lot. I got onto the freeway and entered the flow of traffic. I was trembling. This was way too much exposure. As for the fuck-up, Johnson would be pissed. But I had done what I had to do. He couldn't be pissed at me.

I parked on the far side of the mall and went in looking for Ava. She was sitting near the fountain and smiled when she saw me. Her smile faded and she stood up.

"What's wrong?"

"Nothing. Let's get out of here."

We started for the front entrance. She pulled a couple of ball caps from her purse and showed them to me. One had the logo of the University of Texas and the other that of Texas A&M. We were almost out the door when we heard a masculine voice say "Hold it right there."

We turned to look. It was a mall cop, just another overweight guy in a dead-end job. He approached us all official and in charge.

"Let's see your receipt."

Ava dug in her purse and showed him. He studied it like he was too dumb to read. I put my hand in my pocket and felt the reassuring solidity of the .32.

The guard looked disappointed. "Okay," he said. "It's just that you were buying a Longhorn cap and an Aggie cap. Nobody ever does that. It just looked suspicious."

I wanted to laugh in his face and smash in his face. "Oh yass," said Ava, "veer Cherman. Ve luff Taxes cooltour. Ees correct, Hans?" She looked at me.

"Ja," I said. "Deutsch."

He looked at me like I was the stupid one. "Well which is it, German or Dutch?"

"Cherman. Deutsch," Ava said. "Ees de same. Ees same." She smiled somehow uncertain and reassuring at the same time.

He frowned. "Well, have a nice day."

Back at the car I started laughing and couldn't stop. She laughed with me at first then frowned.

"What happened?" she said.

I caught my breath. "Nothing much."

"How'd it go?"

"Okay."

"Yeah?"

"You'll see."

When we passed through that little town Jewell I told her about my fantasy of robbing both banks at once. She laughed. "That sounds like fun. Let's do it!"

"No."

"Why not?"

"Too dangerous."

When we got back to my place it was late and we were starving. We ordered a pizza and opened a strong red Zinfandel that could stand up to the tomato sauce, pineapple and Italian sausage. She downloaded the footage onto her laptop and plugged it into the TV set. When we got to the part when I pistol whipped the guard, she put down her pizza and covered her mouth with her hand. She paused the video.

"I thought you said you dislike violence," she said.

"I do," I said.

"Doesn't look like it."

"This is the first time that's ever happened," I said. "He was stupid. He had it coming."

She started the video again. When she saw the look on the contact's face, she broke out laughing. I did too. I couldn't help myself.

"Priceless," she said.

"He's fucked," I said.

She looked at me, suddenly serious.

The video kept running. I nearly hit a car on the way out of the parking lot and never even saw it. I pulled off and threw the gun out the window. This was not cool.

I went into the mall and met Ava. "We've got to erase this," I said.

The mall guard came up to us and asked about the hats. The look on his face when he said "which is it, German or Dutch" was too much and we broke out laughing again.

"What a genius," I said at the same time she said, "What a moron." We were laughing like crazy.

I caught my breath. I said, "No, we have to erase that."

"I guess so," she said.

15

The next day I met Virgil at another restaurant. Sitting with him was a soft, fat guy, bald and in glasses. He looked like an accountant. Virgil introduced him as Homer.

"You make a great team, I said.

Homer looked impatient. "We heard about the trouble," he said. He looked at Virgil. "I'll talk to you later," he said.

Virgil took the money and split.

"You agreed to notify us of any trouble," Homer said.

"I didn't have any trouble," I said. "The trouble was all on them."

"We have some exposure here, too," he said.

"Look," I said, "the guard was a fool and your contact was an idiot. He put himself in the shit."

"Be that as it may," he said, "some of that shit may get on us. He's not happy about that."

I knew who he meant.

"This will cause us a good deal of time and effort, and a significant outlay," he said. "The guard's kind of a hero now, and our contact's already in jail."

"Not my problem," I said. "Where do you even get these people?"

He looked a little embarrassed. "He came to us."

I kind of smiled and shook my head.

"We don't like problems," he said. "He won't put up with a problem person."

"I don't know what you want me to do about it."

"It would be far better, in a case like this, if they couldn't testify."

"That's not my line of work."

He smiled. "You know," he said, "as a kind of personal liability insurance."

"I have all the insurance I need."

"We figure you owe us 20 grand."

"How'd you figure?"

"That won't even cover our cost."

"I think we got this straight at the beginning. I'm a contractor, more of a consultant, really. I come in at a critical point in the transaction to perform a highly specialized job for which I am uniquely qualified. You don't want any complications on your end, and neither do I. By rights, I ought to be charging you extra for my time."

He sat there staring at me like a poisonous toad.

"You've made quite a little money with us. You might not find it so easy to line up good jobs in the future, if there is one."

"If this is the kind of job you're lining up, I'll just go back into retirement. If I want to work, there's always someone in need of my services."

"Not in this town. Not in this great state."

I stood up. "Well, nice doing business with you." I said. "Have a nice day."

16

I only saw Ava two or three times in the next couple of weeks. She was spending all of her time writing, she said. What could take so long? I wondered. I mean, how hard could it be?

Seemed like I had more energy than ever. I was working out four hours a day and I didn't feel tired. One day I bicycled 110 miles of Hill Country back roads, a truly epic and liberating ride. Another day, at Barton Springs, I swam 16 quarter-mile laps. Afterward I lay on the grass, and I felt like I could swim 16 more. My body seemed to absorb mystical vibrations from the water and the light and the people and grass and birds and every unseen insect droning in the trees and the trees themselves then to radiate all that back to the universe in rainbow hued harmonies. I glimpsed the order underlying and overarching everything and I was filled with and surrounded by a peace that surpassed all argument and understanding and I understood in that moment that the singular, unitary, undifferentiated original force beyond space and time was love, pure love. The grass, the leaves, the sky glowed with inner fire. A tiny ant crawled on my thumb and I studied the minutest detail of the intricate organization with profound reverence and awe.

A cloud passed over the sun like the blink of an eye. The vibrations relaxed their intensity, the harmonies dropped lower on the scale, a ground tone. I gathered my things and left, walking about two feet off the ground and smiling at everyone I saw. I guess this is why they say Barton Springs is a sacred place.

Austin traffic would try the patience of a saint. Today was more hellacious than ever. As I sat through the third cycle of the light at Fifth and Lamar, I picked up the phone to call her. I wanted to talk to her, see her, touch her, feel her, merge with her in all this sea of love. I noticed it was only one o'clock. She wouldn't pick up. Anyway, if she did, I could hear how the conversation would go.

"I want to see you."

"I'm busy right now."

"Too busy for me?" I know, I sound pathetic. I've never begged for it.

"Honey, baby," she'd say, "I'm writing. I'm deep in this other world, and I don't want to pull out of it now."

"Seems like your imaginary world is more important than the real one."

"You don't understand how much effort it takes to get there, and once there, once I'm really immersed in the characters' lives, in their world, if I'm pulled out of it, well, it's just really hard to get back. You know?"

"Well, what's happening in their world?"

"I don't want to talk it away. I can't talk right now. I'll call you tonight."

Unless she was on a roll, in which case, I wouldn't hear from her and she wouldn't pick up.

When I got home I knew I should eat something but I wasn't even hungry. I managed to choke down a banana. I took a shower and afterward stood there looking at myself in the mirror. I was lean and cut and bursting with health. What woman wouldn't want to be with me?

I started drinking beer and quickly ran through the six-pack, but I didn't feel the least bit drunk. I shifted over to tequila—a premium brand, of course, but, frankly, it's all cactus juice. Continuous applications were required to get me through the back-to-back stupid movies on TV. I woke up in the middle of the night not remembering how I got to bed; I had a raging headache and boner so hard I could have stuck it in a knothole. I wanted every woman I've ever wanted, but I couldn't think of any woman but her. I reached down and grabbed ahold to bring me some relief, but even that felt like being unfaithful. I tossed and turned and groveled and groaned and whined like a whipped puppy. I almost prayed to god. I was the most pathetic loser on the planet.

Who knows how long I writhed on my bed of pain? Later I drank some water and ate part of a soft-boiled egg. I felt stupid and guilty. There was only one cure.

I opened the secret stash and got out the bottle, an unopened ounce of pharmaceutical grade cocaine. This was not your every day hipster crap, but one hundred percent scientifically pure, the magic powder of Sigmund Freud and Keith Richards. I took two tiny spoonsful up each nostril—instant relief. My headache was gone, and I felt a lot better about myself. The day took on the rosy glow of possibility.

I picked up my guitar and played for a good hour. I could do no wrong. I went to some mad places. When my concentration started fuzzing out, I thought of what good work I could do if I took a couple more sniffs. But that way lay disaster and insanity. No wonder it's illegal, or rather a controlled substance, available only by prescription and under strict medical supervision with government oversight of the practitioners. Truly, cocaine should only be administered by those capable of the utmost self-control.

I ate some fruit and got on the bicycle. I rode west to the hills and burned up the steepest I could find. Hours later I came home wringing wet and took a cold shower. I went to bed and took a nap. The phone woke me.

I went to the other room. It was Ava.

"Hi baby," I said.

"Hi," she said. "What's up?"

"Nothing," I said. "Just woke up from a nap."

"Sounds nice."

"What's up with you?"

"I've kind of hit a wall here."

I waited.

"I'm just tired. I'm feeling cooped up. I'm going a little crazy."

"Why don't you come over? I'll fix you some supper."

"That sounds nice. Want me to pick up anything?"

"No, I've got it covered."

I sniffed a couple of lines—I didn't want to flag now. I opened a nice cabernet sauvignon to let it breathe and prepped some lamb chops with broccoli and new potatoes—simple and delicious. Ava came in looking so simple and fresh and beautiful I took her in my arms and gave her a long hug and a big kiss. She pulled away and walked around the room touching things. "Care for some wine?" I said.

"Oh," she said, as if the question surprised her, "yes, thanks."

I poured her a glass and she took an automatic sip, like she was someplace else. "Something the matter?" I said.

"No, nothing," she said. "Never mind."

We ate, and afterward I was sitting on the couch enjoying my wine while she flitted about the living room like a butterfly, kind of bouncing off the walls, really.

"Want to talk about it?" I said.

"No," she said quickly. She stopped and stared at me. "I have been preoccupied, haven't I? I'm trying not to think about it, but it just keeps churning away in there." She smacked herself on the side of the head and made a funny face. "I just need to think about something else."

"Come here," I said.

She came into my arms. I took her to bed and gave her something else to think about.

17

I like to watch the neighborhood cats. Do you ever watch the cats? I like to think I understand them pretty well. I think of myself as something of a cat psychologist. Basically, cats are sociopaths.

I was sitting in my garden in the cool of the morning. I bet I didn't sleep an hour and a half yet here I was wide awake and raring to go. I took a sip of my cooling coffee. Ava was sleeping in blissful oblivion. I was watching the cats.

The tuxedo across the street was creeping through the neighbor's cactus patch unfazed by the needles and thorns. A cute little calico stalked something in the bunch grass and stopped to study a bird on a low branch. The lop-eared tabby was busy conserving energy while closely watching the calico—let her do the hunting for him, I guessed. Then along came the monster boss cat of the neighborhood. He was a really dark tiger—you could only see his markings in certain lights—and he must have weighed 25 pounds. The other cats went belly down when he strode through on stiff legs. He was as nice as a cat can be. He loved to be petted. He rubbed up against my legs and purred. A real con man.

Cats seem so lovable and cute, but they're probably not capable of feeling such a complicated emotion as love. They make you love them, but they don't love you back. Cats divide the world into two things—sources of food, and everything else. You're too big to be prey. But cats are smart. They've figured out that you are a potential resource. So they manipulate you. Cats have other needs, as well—water, and some degree of protection from predators, chiefly other cats. You can provide both. And if they desire a little rubbing and petting and scratching behind the ears, well, you might be a likely candidate.

Indeed, unlike any other animal, cats have domesticated people

Ava came out with a tray, a mug and a pot of coffee, looking pretty bleary and smeary. I wondered what she'd look like in 15 or 20 years.

She set the tray on the table, sat on my lap and gave me a sweet little kiss. "Last night," she said, "you were so passionate."

"I missed you," I said. "I want you with me all the time."

She moved to the other chair and poured a cup of coffee. I tossed out the dregs of my cup and happily accepted a refill.

"I love your garden," she said.

"Yeah," I said, "it brings me a lot of peace."

She studied me. "You're a strange person," she said.

"What do you mean?"

"You talk of peace, yet you're prone to violence."

"What do you mean?"

"That was pretty scary, what you did to that guy. And when you pick up his gun and you have him in your sights, I can really see your struggle. Your hands are shaking. You really wanted to shoot him, didn't you?"

"What are you talking about?"

"The video."

"You were supposed to erase that."

"I will. But I have to study it first. It's really scary."

We sat there enjoying our coffee, the morning birdsongs and the pretty flowers like any other couple.

"I meant what I said," I said.

"I said I'll erase it," she said.

"Not that," I said. "Well, yes, that, but I was talking about the other. I want you here, with me, all the time."

I could see the wheels turning, like she was trying to make up excuses.

"I mean it," I said. "If that is a change of status or taking it to the next level, if it's a proposal, that's what I'm talking about. I'm willing to go all the way."

"No," she said, "I can't think about that right now. It's too much of a distraction. I need to focus on the script."

"Why is it taking so long?"

"I want it to be good. You want it to be good. You're paying me good money."

So now she was throwing that in my face. "What kind of progress are you making?"

"It's hard to say."

"Seems like a simple enough thing. You write a certain number of pages a day, and after a certain number of days…"

"It doesn't work like that. Some days I might write ten or even twenty pages, others maybe one. Some days I write five or ten good pages and the next day I come back and erase it all. Maybe the scenes are even good but they're taking the story to a place it doesn't want to go. Some days maybe I'll write nothing. I'll just wander around from room to room or maybe I'll draw pictures and charts and diagrams or who knows what.

"Well, why do you have to write it?" I said. "Why don't we hire someone?"

"This is my vision. This is my movie. I'm the author."

I looked at the cats, then back at her.

She put her hand on my arm. "Honey, baby, Alex." She sounded like my mother. "You only get one chance to be a first time filmmaker. If—and I mean if—anyone even notices your film, your path is pretty well set. If it does well, they'll trust you enough to make another one. If not, not."

"I'd trust you."

"You're sweet."

The cats were circling.

"By the way," she said, "I have some payments coming up and I need to do some maintenance on my car and…"

"You need what?" I said, "Another ten?"

"Yeah, I guess. That should do."

"Just a second." I went inside and back to my bedroom. I took a stack of hundreds from the dresser drawer. I started back and there she was, right outside, in the hall. So now she knew where I kept the cash.

"I didn't know if you wanted me to wait, or…," she said.

"Here." I handed her the money.

"Sorry. I mean thanks," she said.

I walked her to her car. I held the door for her while she got in. I stooped to the window and she gave me her cheek to kiss.

"When are you going on another job?" she said.

"I'm not."

"Why not?"

"I don't want to. I don't need it," I said. "The other day, that nearly got out of control."

She pressed her lips into a thin line.

"Call me," I said.

"I will," she said.

She drove away. I went back to the cats.

18

I received a text from an attorney named Diaz. This time the meet was in an upscale sushi bar. That made me a bit apprehensive.

I got there early, but I was anticipated. I don't know what I was expecting, but it sure wasn't this.

She gave me a scented and embossed card: "Beatriz Diaz del Castillo, Attorney at Law." With the same motion, she rose and extended her hand as if for a kiss. Her fingers were long and thin, the nails painted bright red. The color matched that of her curvaceous lips, which parted in a sultry smile as she looked me over. Her eyes were deep and dark; her skin was fair; her nose could have been Maya or Aztec. Her black and white dress seemed too tight. I wondered how it could be sewn to fit her tiny waist and exaggerated hips and breasts.

Next to her, I felt underdressed. I had worn a silk t-shit, linen slacks and sandals, with a lightweight blazer because I needed a pocket for my pistol.

Still, there was something not quite right about her. Despite the designer labels, the flawless make-up, the $400 haircut, there was something a bit forced and inelegant. She was trying too hard to look the part of the femme fatale.

We ordered the special—various kinds of sashimi and miso soup. She had sake, and I had a beer.

"Mr. Hardy," she said. "We want to offer you an apology."

"Oh?"

"Mr. Homer was not in fact an employee of ours. He was in fact colluding with our employee to divert company resources and use our good name and network of contacts to redirect revenues into their own pockets." She had just the faintest hint of an accent.

"I see."

"Yes, any time your company grows beyond just a handful of employees, corruption, embezzlement, employee theft, call it what you will, becomes a problem."

"I imagine."

"Yes, it's so very unpleasant." She smiled briefly. "I have been instructed to inform you that Mr. Virgil is no longer in our employ."

"And Homer?"

"I believe he has relocated, possibly out of state," she said.

Our lunch arrived. "I do so prefer sashimi to sushi, don't you?"

"I haven't really thought about it."

"I don't care for the seaweed and all that rice," she said. "I love the pure taste of the fish just as it came from the water—just as it is, natural, and raw, and…" she lowered her voice "…naked."

She put a piece of tuna in her mouth and made a show of savoring it. "So sweet, so rich, with just that hint of astringency." Her eyes were molten.

I took a bite. "Delicious," I said.

"Yes," she said. "It tastes like the sea." Her eyes were dark as the depths. She took another bite with exaggerated sensuality. She almost purred.

The thing about lunch is, it's not a date. It has a natural beginning, middle and end. I pulled out some cash. She picked up the check and said, "We'll let my client get this."

The waitress took her card. "It's been a great pleasure meeting you," she said. The card came back and she signed. "My client tells me your relationship has been very profitable for him, and he believes that the same is true for you."

"He does?"

"Mutually satisfying, yes? He wishes to continue contracting your services, from time to time, as mutually agreeable."

"I'll think about it."

"Thank you. In the future, you may direct all communications to me. I am to make sure all your needs are taken care of."

I looked her over good this time, and let her know I was looking. She preened and posed. There was something not quite right about that black and white dress of hers. The geometry of the print was wrong somehow, like she had no eye for style, or maybe she bought the dress in a thrift shop and reworked it to fit her overstated figure. She sort of leaned forward and pulled her arms together, giving me a good long look at her assets.

"Thanks," I said.

"I look forward to working more closely with you," she said. "Soon, I hope."

As we walked out together she kept bumping her boob and hip against me. As we waited for the valets to bring our cars, she was rubbing that stuff all over me. Her car came, a cute little Mercedes two-seater. She showed me a lot of thigh getting behind the wheel. She waved and drove away just as my car was coming.

She was a hell of a woman all right, but definitely not my type. Still, I figured, before all was said and done, I would probably have to fuck her.

19

I called Ava. No answer.

I decided to do a line of coke and spend a few hours in the studio. After that first one, I thought what the hell and did another. This stuff was really smooth and not jittery at all.

Well, it took me to some pretty out-of-the-way places. I have this vintage Gibson amp—an antique, really—that makes a really spooky sound when you turn the volume all the way down and the reverb all the way up, and I had a distortion pedal going through that. I was thinking how cool that would sound on one of Geoff's songs, but it wasn't the kind of thing you could do live very well and anyway I didn't want to gig with that amp.

In one of those crazy cocaine coincidences, the phone rang. Geoff had lined up a few gigs and he wanted to rehearse. "Cool," I said.

The boys would be at my place right after supper. I hadn't eaten all day. I made myself eat a soft-boiled egg and half a piece of toast. I could feel the coke wearing off and I didn't want to flag, so I did another couple of lines.

They arrived pretty much on time for musicians. These must be good-paying gigs, I figured, because Geoff had brought Randy. We stood around in the kitchen a few minutes chatting. They passed around a pipe and I declined. I didn't want to mess up my head. I poured a couple of fingers of a peaty single malt. When your mouth is all alive from the coke, that shit tastes insane.

We hit the studio and got to work. I wanted to wrap this up at ten. My studio is fairly well sound-proofed, but you can feel the thump of that bass drum right through the wall. I get along with my neighbors, and I want to keep getting along with them.

We plowed through a set of old familiars, then Geoff showed us a couple of new numbers he'd written, and we ended up stretching out on a cover of an old '70s rocker we'd never done before—a simple, three-chord song, but we caught a groove and actually sounded pretty good. Randy's one of those players who lifts all the players around him and makes them sound better than they are. On keys, he brings a whole new palette of tonal colors. But to call him a keyboard player does him a disservice; he's a great all-round musician. On that last tune he picked up my Strat and we ripped out a long interweaving instrumental like Clapton and Winwood or Stills and Young, not that I could play with those cats but we touched that rarefied ether a time or two.

Geoff and I sat around talking and drinking after the others left. We're the only ones that don't have day jobs—Randy's a bona fide professor. We both thought we sounded good. Geoff thought we should make a record—as a marketing tool for the band, and to help promote his songs. That sounded good to me. It would give me a chance to spend some money. Studio time ain't cheap, and those guys would be more than happy to take cash. It all went through the band anyway, and Geoff owned the band. I was just a paid employee even though I paid for it all.

After Geoff split, I faced that moment all users of cocaine must face: Do another bump, or continue the comedown. This is the moment that separates the rational person who carefully controls a performance enhancing prescription, and the insane addict who ends up trying to cut the bugs out of his skin.

I checked my phone. Ava had called. I decided it would serve her right to have to wait till tomorrow, maybe restore some balance to our relationship. I went to bed with a book, and was able to sleep toward dawn.

I texted her a little before noon and she called me right back. I guess my inattention got her attention. She asked me to come over for lunch. She greeted me at the door wearing pearl earrings, a matching necklace, and nothing else. A couple of hours later and we still hadn't eaten.

"Are you hungry?" she said.

"Not really," I said.

"I'm starving," she said.

We got dressed and went to the neighborhood taqueria. I had some of the chips and salsa and a carne guisada taco I couldn't finish. I sat there and watched her wolf an entire cheese enchilada dinner, and felt faintly disgusted.

We were waiting for the check. "I'm feeling kind of blocked," she said.

"Well, when you eat like that," I said.

She laughed. "Not like that." She frowned. "When are you going on another job?" she said.

"I'm not," I said.

"I'm really stuck," she said. "I just can't get the realism I want because I don't know enough. I need to do more research."

"I told you," I said.

"What about those people?"

"I don't think I'm going to work with them any more."

"Why not?"

"I'm not sure I can trust them."

I left the money on the table. On the way to my place, she started in on me again. "Honey, baby," she said, "Alex, we have a lot of time and effort and money in this already. Don't you want me to succeed?"

That was unfair. "Of course."

"I'm sorry. It's just that... Oh, never mind."

We rode in silence for a few blocks.

"You wouldn't understand," she said.

I figured silence was better than any rejoinder I could make. We got home and she took me straight to bed. She worked me over from head to foot. She was really knocking herself out. I gave as good as I got, of course. If anyone had heard her screaming they would have called the cops. Later, as she was riding me, her eyes rolled back in her head, I was thinking about our relationship and I realized in a moment of clarity that there was something conditional in her love for me.

Still later we snacked on prosciutto, cheese and honeydew. She was searching one of the on-line services and pulled up Dog Day Afternoon. "If I can't see first hand, I'll have to get my ideas from the most realistic crime dramas I can find," she said.

"I've never seen it," I said.

"I can't believe you've never seen it," she said.

"Me neither," I said.

What can I say? It's a true classic. If you haven't seen it, you should.

"I just love the grit and the realism," she said.

"I liked it," I said, "but I wouldn't call it realistic. Not the crime part. The part about the cops, that's pretty real."

"What do you mean?"

"I mean the way they murder the guy in custody."

"He's not in custody."

"They could have disarmed him easy. He was probably retarded."

"Well, what was wrong with the crime?"

"No one would do that. It's nothing like that. It's not like that at all."

"See, that's why I need you to take me along on a job."

"No." I was rather enjoying this. I could see it made her more ardent.

We went back to bed and she was all over me again. Afterward, she passed out. I lay there studying her face in the light seeping in through the blinds. What was it about this particular woman that I wanted her to spend the rest of her life with me? In sleep, she looked so young and innocent, yet in her unguarded, unconscious state you could see age had set its teeth and claws into her face. Her hair fanned out on the pillow. Was it rich and full-bodied, or merely coarse? I distinctly saw hints of silver glinting among the multicolored strands. I realized I had never asked about her ethnicity. She could have had some Mexican in her, maybe some Native American or African-American, possibly Chinese or Japanese, for that matter. She had an otherworldly, cosmopolitan face. She could even have been from another time, like ancient Rome or Sumeria.

No one ever asks about me, even though my mother was Cuban. I'm about as white as they come.

We woke together. She took me firmly in hand. "I love waking up with you," she said.

We kissed and cuddled and fondled. She was starting to go down on me.

"If you won't show me," she said, "I guess I'll just have to try something myself."

"No," I said.

"You don't want me to?" she said. "I thought you liked it."

"No, I mean I'm not going to let you do something stupid."

"You can refuse to help me," she said. "That's your right. But you can't stop me from doing something stupid if I want to." She had me there.

"Let me think," I said.

We left it at that but I didn't do anything like thinking for quite a while. Then she showered and dressed and I drove her home. When we stopped in front of her place, she leaned over and gave me a sexy kiss.

"What about that little town on the interstate?" she said. "The one with two banks? You said that would be fun."

"I said, let me think about it."

20

We got rolling on the record project and that took up a lot of my time. We were rehearsing three or four times a week, so when we went into the studio we were ready. We were trying to do this recording as live as possible. I don't know if you're aware, but most of the records you listen to were recorded one part at a time. Your principal cuts a scratch-track maybe, with vocal and guitar or piano, or somebody lays down a rhythm track, then each player plays his part separately while listening to playback on headphones. It can be tedious, frustrating and not much fun. In the end, you get everything sounding perfect. But sometimes it's too perfect.

There's a certain spirit, a certain feel, that can happen when musicians are accustomed to playing together, a certain unspoken interactive consciousness that can lift the music to a higher level. That's what we were going for.

You'd think recording live would be a lot easier and more fun. You just go in and play the song, right? But that's not necessarily the case. Because of the bleed from one sound source to the next you can't go back and fix mistakes, and because all of you are playing at the same time everybody has to get it right at the same time. That means you go in and play the song over and over and over until you get a performance you like. I remember reading somewhere that Tom Petty's "Refugee" required something like 125 takes. We're not The Heartbreakers, but sometimes it felt like it. Big Don couldn't or wouldn't play to a click track in his headphones, and Skinny Don always seemed to be lagging, when you need that bass to step right in there and define the beat. I don't know why I never noticed before. I guess when you're playing live nobody is really paying that much attention.

When you get stuck, you just have to take a break. I went out to the car and took a couple of toots out of my little bullet-shaped traveler, just to settle me down. It wouldn't do any good to get mad, but man I would love to smash a couple of guitars and give those guys a swift kick in the ass.

Then one morning I got up and noticed that my little bottle was less than a quarter full. That wouldn't do. I called my contact. I called Geoff and told him I had to go out of town for two or three days. I threw a t-shirt and a pair of underwear in a bag, put some trail mix in a zip-lock, filled a one liter water bottle, carefully transferred the rest of the coke into my bullet, fired up the Beamer and hit the highway.

My contact had a very exclusive clientele. With all the attention on the cartels, most people don't even know such things exist, but you could guess his partner was in quality control at the only licensed manufacturer of pharmaceutical cocaine in America. He could pull bottles off the line for any reason.

I cruised our country's wonderful, if aging, system of interstate highways, originally designed of course for the military, always the top priority. This epic driving was a return to my past; I was back to my old system. I stopped only for gas, to pee, and, occasionally, to admire a scenic vista. I nibbled the odd handful of trail mix, or I would put one piece of beef jerky in my mouth and hold it there, swallowing the juice, until it was soft enough to mash up with my tongue. I could make one piece last half an hour that way. I took one snort from my traveler up one nostril once every four hours, first the right, then four hours later the left, as needed. I never got stoned or loaded or high, but I never got sleepy or tired and my attention never flagged.

After 22 hours I reached a mid-sized city in an unnamed Midwestern state. I showered at a truck stop and changed my underwear. I texted my contact and met him at an apartment downtown.

He pulled out an ounce and I sat there thinking. "Why not make it a couple," I said.

"Okay," he said.

"On second thought," I said, "make it five."

Drug dealers know not to comment on their customer's usage, but he looked at me kind of funny.

"Save me a trip," I said.

"Sure," he said. "See you next time."

"Thanks," I said. I refilled my bullet, locked the bottles in the trunk, and I was back on the road. I was careful to set my cruise control exactly five miles over the limit; some of these cops will pull you over on suspicion if you're traveling at the posted speed.

All that driving gave me a chance to think. Oh I listened to music and I had an audio book, but most of the time I turned it all off and communed with silence, just me and the quiet whoosh of the road.

Of course, I loved Ava, loved her with all my heart, her and only her, but she was trying to use sex to get her way. Why do women always want to turn the bed into a bargaining table? I've always thought sex was about two people showing how much they love each other, or at least two people enjoying each other's company in this uniquely beautiful way. But women always seem to make it into a transaction.

I got to thinking about that movie she liked. It was really ahead of its time, with the homosexual and transsexual themes. I suddenly wondered about Ava, about why she liked that movie so much. There was something masculine and aggressive about her, the way she ran that film set, that I found attractive at the time. But the way she insisted on having her own way about the script, well, I was getting tired of it. Now if she was trans, and we were doing it, what would that say about me? Nah, she was all woman all right, but then again the surgeons could do amazing things. I would have to look closely at her hands; their hands give them away.

Then for some reason I got to thinking about Beatriz. She looked so awkward and inelegant in that get-up I had to shake my head. It was almost cute, like a five-year-old playing dress-up. The more I thought about it the more I was sure she had bought that dress in a thrift shop and altered it. She just didn't look right in it. On the other hand, I bet she looked good out of it. I chuckled. She would be everyman's fantasy of impossible architecture and cantilevered curves.

Ava. Beatriz. Beatriz. Ava. One from Column A and one from Column B. There could be no comparison. Ava was intelligent, creative, driven, competent, proficient and accomplished. Beatriz was built for the bedroom.

When I crossed the Red River into Texas, I still had a long way to go. I tweeted a little celebratory toot out of sequence. Truth was, after 40 hours I was starting to lose my edge.

I wanted to drive straight through but south of Waco I had to pee. I exited the freeway and realized I was in that little town Jewell. Well, it was no jewel, hardly a town at all, just a few metal buildings and houses plopped in the middle of a cotton field with a little bank on both sides of the interstate. I pulled into the parking lot the western bank shared with a gas station and a grocery store. I went into the gas station to use the bathroom and bought a liter of water. I circled past the bank to get on the freeway and looked it over pretty good. It looked like a whole lot of nothing. I drove a few miles south and exited at a little farm road, then drove back north and checked out the bank on the east side. There was no need to slow down—there was nothing to see. I continued north a few miles, exited, turned around and headed home.

As I drove through the town one last time, I firmly dismissed the idea. Without thinking, I kind of automatically took a little toot and realized right after I didn't want to. Now it would take me a little longer to come down. Oh well, maybe it would ease the descent.

21

I got home about dark. When I got out of the car, I was walking like a cripple. I ran a tub of cold water. I brought a big bowl of ice into the bathroom and eased myself into the tub. After I got used to the temperature, I added ice and lay back. After chilling for a while I drained the water and took a warm shower. I looked in the ice box—the thought of food was revolting. I drank a small cup of milk and went to bed. I lay there for a long time practicing self-control. By keeping still, careful breathing and various meditative techniques, I was eventually able to fall asleep, a twilight sleep at first, but then I truly slept.

I woke up at first light starving. I went to the taqueria for huevos y frijoles. I went home and went back to bed and slept until dark. I woke up thinking about Beatriz, of all people. I doubted she even was an attorney. She couldn't be 30. How could a woman that looked like that end up working for someone like Johnson? Of course—she was a high-priced whore. When I thought about how, and why, she would have turned to prostitution, well, I felt sorry for her.

I got up and called Ava.

"Have you eaten?" she said. "Come on over."

I went right over.

"I made gazpacho," she said.

The cold soup was just the thing for summer, and there was some nice bread and an acceptable wine.

She gave me a girlish smile. I could tell what she was thinking.

"How's the script coming?" I said.

"Great! I'm almost finished."

"When will it be ready?"

"Another week or so. Depending." She gave me a significant look. I thought I understood her significance, but I pretended otherwise. I don't like being controlled or manipulated.

"Great! I want to read it."

"You can't."

"Huh?"

"Nobody reads my script."

"What?"

"No."

"Don't the actors have to?"

"I'll tell them what they need to know when they need to know it. You can't trust actors."

"Wow, I guess I got that wrong. I thought they'd have to, you know, memorize their lines."

"That's not how I'm working. It's mostly improv."

"But what about me? Why can't I read it? Don't you want some, you know, feedback?"

"No. I don't want anyone second guessing me." Her intensity sharpened the lines of her face and made her look suddenly old. "Look, this is a working document. More like notes to myself, really. Everything's fluid, everything's subject to change. I don't want anyone, even myself, having too fixed an idea about what's happening. We need feel that everyday uncertainty about what's coming next, you know, we need to feel the true uncertainty of life."

"Okay, well what is happening next?"

"Have you given any more thought to, you know?"

"Yeah."

"And?"

"It could be done," I said, "but it wouldn't be worth it. There couldn't be more than four or five thousand there."

"You said you don't need the money."

"I'll set something up, like before."

"No. You were right. That was boring. I want to see some real action. You know, a real adrenaline rush."

"I thought you wanted it real."

"Yeah, crazy real."

She came around the table, sat in my lap and stuck her tongue in my mouth. She led me by the hand to the bedroom, and, for a long time, time stood still. We went at it backwards and forwards, this way and that, upside down and sideways. At one point she kicked me in the head and I just kept on laughing. I was working with all my might, straining and striving, and suddenly flashed into my mind the image of Beatriz.

I flopped over on my back, breathing hard. Ava cuddled up next to me. But it was Beatriz I was thinking of.

22

The next day, Beatriz called. She wanted me to meet her at her office. Her office was in her house. She lived in the hills not too far to the west.

She greeted me at the door. Her skimpy little dress barely covered her assets, and in those platform heels she looked like she was about to topple over. She showed me into the living room, which was furnished with a desk and chairs, a love seat by the window and a beautiful oriental rug. "Nice carpet," I said.

"Yes, it's Chinese," she said, "pure silk." The way she said "silk" was, like, wow.

She sat on the love seat. "I believe," she said, "communication is the soul of any relationship, whether business or personal. Don't you agree?"

"Definitely," I said.

I sat next to her. Within two minutes I had her down on the floor with her dress around her neck and her legs in the air. That carpet really was silk.

Once again, I'm not the kind to kiss and tell. But I have never met anyone as passionate as Beatriz. She put her entire heart and soul into the act. She was incredibly giving, and she obviously got a lot in return. She screamed, she whimpered, she moaned, she laughed, she cried, sometimes she laughed and cried at the same time. She shook, she shivered, she trembled, she quivered and quaked. She told me how good every part of me looked, felt, sounded, tasted and smelled. She begged and pleaded and sweet-talked. She lavished attention over every square inch of my skin, something like 2,880, and aroused and excited all 54 some-odd million sensory receptors. Her skills were professional level. We did everything we could do and then some. We sprawled all over the floor.

After a while she took me by the hand and led me to her bed and we started in all over again. I thought I had done a pretty good number on her— her hair was tangled, her lipstick smeared and her eyeliner running down her face—but somehow she was still kind of half wearing her bra. I started to take it off.

"No," she said. That was the first time she said no to me.

"Take it off," I said.

"No," she said.

"Why not?" I said.

"I don't want to," she said.

This was ridiculous. She had everything on display except for this narrow band of elastic, the cups pushed down and the straps around her elbows. "What's the matter, are they fake?"

"No." She stuck out her lower lip and pouted like a five-year-old. For some reason, that just pissed me off.

"Do it," I said.

She actually started to cry. That made me all the more determined to make her do what I told her. I pinched her in a sensitive place.

"Now," I said.

She hung her head and her hair covered her face as she reached around and undid the hooks. Those massive things spilled out and flopped and bounced and swayed. She tried to cover them up and control them with her hands. "Let me see," I said. I lifted each separately and carefully examined the underside. "No scars," I said.

She was still pouting.

"Now what was so bad about that?" I said.

She kept looking down with her hair in her face.

"Answer me," I said. "And look at me when you speak."

Her eyes were big and frightened and full of tears. "They're too big," she said.

I laughed. "You're joking," I said. "Some things, they just can't hardly be too big."

"But," she lifted them, "they sag."

I was still laughing as I pulled her down on the bed and started stroking them. "Honey baby, anything that big is going to sag a little."

"You like them?" she said in a quiet little voice.

"I love them," I said. I was only exaggerating a little.

That's when I discovered she had a curious—unique in my experience— anatomical feature. I was pretty well worn out, spent and depleted, if you know what I mean, but even so she was able seemed like to reach out with that little thing of hers and grab hold and drag me in and work me over until lo and behold I was raring to go again.

After a while I realized time was passing and I had to meet the guys in the studio. I sat up and waited for my head to clear.

"Sweetheart?" she said. She started pulling me down, back into her arms.

"I gotta go," I said.

She started touching and kissing and working on me till I had to give it to her again. I jumped out of bed as soon as I was done. She lay there watching me and touching herself as I got dressed. "I'm meeting some people," I said. "I don't want to be late."

Her eyes were all iris. She looked at me like how could anything be more important than this. I gave her a final kiss, untangled her arms, and left without another word.

I went by the house to pick up my guitar. I was so tired I did a couple of lines in each nostril.

She made me late. That pissed me off. I called her early the next morning and told her I was coming over to punish her. She was wearing a dress even shorter than the day before and, as I immediately verified, nothing underneath. In seconds I had it pushed up and pulled down. "This is your punishment," I said.

She made me punish her all afternoon. When I was getting ready to leave I said, "Don't make me late," I said, "unless you want me to punish you like that again."

"Please?" she said. So I had to punish her some more before I could get away, and I was late again. It was a vicious cycle.

There was something about her that brought out something in me. I wanted to make her do whatever I wanted her to whether she wanted to or not. But clearly, she was making me do things she wanted me to do.

I was over there every day that week, and in the studio evenings. I needed a little boost, if you know what I mean.

Every day I went over there she was wearing a sexier outfit, ridiculous fantasy stuff that looked best on the bedroom floor. One day she almost had on a barely there bikini, which didn't make it to the pool. We did it beside the pool, we did it in the pool, we did it in the hot tub. We did it in the bedroom, in the bathroom, the living room and the kitchen. We did it in the guest bedroom, in a third bedroom that was used for storage and was full of boxes, and in the hall half-bath. Then we did it in the garage.

One day I was lying there sprawled out on the bed and she was sprawled out on me and she started making these little kisses on my belly and I knew that I wasn't man enough to rise to the occasion. I felt around and found my pants beside the bed and groped in the pocket and got my little bullet. I took a couple of good blasts. She was watching me with those deep brown eyes. I prepped a hit and passed her the piece. She took it without question or comment. I knew then I had her where I wanted her.

We soared to new heights on the strength of the pharmaceuticals. We did it all day the next day and the day after that. I felt something growing slow.

Something about the way she submitted to my every whim and still got everything she wanted made me want to punish her, but there was only one way to punish her and that was no real punishment at all.

I started thinking about Ava. Ava was going places. She was the one I loved and wanted to spend the rest of my life with.

I noticed Beatriz didn't have much to do except lie around the house with me all day. I may have said something without thinking.

"I have very few clients," she said. "In fact, right now, only one."

"But he pays you very well," I said.

"Yes."

"I think I get it."

Her eyes swam. I was enjoying this.

"He isn't paying you?"

"Not for this."

I got dressed and left. The whole time, she followed me with those deep, swimming eyes.

23

I went home and decided to bag the evening. I picked up my phone and saw it was dead. I wondered how long since I had even thought of it. I had been a bit preoccupied of late.

I plugged in the charger and saw that Ava had called several times. I called Geoff and told him I had a headache, which was true, and had to beg off. I did a couple of maintenance lines and soaked in a hot bath. My body ached all over.

I went outside with a tumbler of Scotch. I needed to relax. It was the crepuscular hour. The cats were circling, the doves were cooing like crazy and the mosquitos were whining, too. I was slapping mosquitos and cats were rubbing up against me. Some of these cats I'd never seen before. They were purring and meowing like they wanted something from me and I didn't have anything for them. I was cussing the cats and slapping mosquitos and they just kept on purring and whining and rubbing even when I kicked them. Crepuscular cats! Finally I said fuck it and gulped down the whiskey and went inside.

I went to bed. I didn't sleep, but I lay perfectly still while the night rolled on. The cats and mosquitoes were locked outside, but the cries and croaks of the night birds came through the walls. I think maybe I did sleep, a little, right at dawn.

I realized I was starving. There was nothing in the refrigerator. I dragged myself to the taqueria for huevos rancheros, but, no matter how hungry I felt, I could only force down a little of the egg yolk dabbed on a corner of corn tortilla. I went home and took a small spoonful up each nostril and instantly felt better.

I called Ava. "How's it going, baby?" I said.

"Where have you been?"

"My phone died."

"Why didn't you stop by?"

"I've been busy. I figured you were busy or you'd call. Nobody calls me anyway."

"I called."

"Except you."

"What's happening?"

"Nothing much. I think we're in the studio tonight. What about you?

How's the script?"

"I've taken it about as far as I can at this point."

I could tell she was waiting for me to say something. I thought I knew what it was.

"So, can I see you?" she said.

"Sure, of course," I said. "Say, let's go swimming."

"Okay. When?"

"I'll be there as soon as I can." I took my own sweet time. You realize it was about a five-minute drive to her place. I got there an hour later. I rather enjoyed making her wait.

I gave her a quick peck and bundled her into the car. She kept looking at me funny on the drive down to Barton Springs. We paid and went inside and she didn't say a word. We spread out our beach towels on the lawn. She lay in the shade of a pecan while I swam my laps. I felt pretty sluggish. It had been a long time since I had worked out. Unless you counted this entire last week. That was quite a workout. I caught myself thinking of Beatriz and getting hard even in that cold water. For just one moment I almost thought that I might like Beatriz better because Ava was too bossy. I kicked up my pace and forced the thought away.

I felt tired after only a half a mile. I got out of the pool and flopped down on my towel next to her. I may have slept. After a while I looked over at her and saw she was lying on her side staring at me.

"Why do you have to be so good looking?" she said.

"I take after my mother," I said.

I may well have been asleep. I was hot and dry and was starting to sweat.

"Don't you want to go in?" I said.

"Isn't this the place where the water is cold?" she said.

"Yeah," I said.

"I told you that other place was cold enough for me."

She was trying to assert control, I realized. "Okay," I said. "Well, I'm going to jump back in and then we can go."

I jumped in and splashed around and dove down to the bottom a couple of times, then got out and started drying off. I shook like a dog and scattered droplets on her. She just sat there staring at me. The more cheerful I acted, the less she became. I was enjoying this.

"Ready?" I said.

Women think they're better at picking up on emotions than men. They may be right about most men, but not me. I can usually tell what other people are thinking and feeling. I get that from my mother. She was practically clairvoyant.

We went back to her place. As soon as she shut the door I dragged her to the bedroom and gave her what she really wanted. They all want the same thing.

Afterward I lay back and stared at the ceiling fan. She cuddled up next to me and started stroking my chest hair. "Honey?" she said. "Baby?"

"Hmm?" I petted her hand.

"I need to go look that place over so I can finalize my plans," she said.

"Your plans?" I said. "What plans?"

"For that scene, you know, in that little town."

"That's not a scene, it's a robbery." I looked at her like she was dumb. "Why are you making the plans? I'm the robber."

"I'm the director." She glared fiercely. "This will be the climactic scene. It requires a lot of planning."

"What do you know about robbery?"

"That's what I need you for."

I tried to look surprised and offended.

"Not only for that," she said.

"How are you doing for money?" I said.

She flinched. "Actually, I will be needing some. I'm ready to start casting."

"Well, let's go get some." We went to my place. I got her a stack of hundreds. I had to be in the studio in an hour so I grabbed my guitar and took her home. On the way, I said, "Look, I've already shown my face in that town, and I don't want to be seen again."

"I'll give you a beard," she said.

"I don't want to take my car, and yours would be the only hybrid in the county. Why don't you try to rent something like a pickup or SUV? Or at least get the plainest car you can find."

"Okay."

"I'll call you in the morning."

I called her early. She came over in a silver minivan. I had to laugh. "Perfect," I said.

She opened her make-up case and gave me a beard with a lot of gray in it. I looked 20 years older. "What about you?" I said.

She smiled. "Okay," she said. She went to the bathroom and started graying her hair. I put on baggy shorts, sandals, white crew socks with red and blue stripes around the top, and that Longhorn baseball cap. When she saw me in that get up she busted out laughing. "You look perfect," she said. "Very patriotic."

She had brushed a lot of gray into her hair. She looked so thoroughly middle-aged that I had to wonder again just how old she was. But, in her tight t-shirt and jeans, she was way too noticeable. "No one will ever believe you're with me," I said. "You need to put on 40 or 50 pounds."

I pulled out a couple of old fanny packs, stuffed them with socks and put them on her fore and aft. She put on a pair of my sweat pants and cinched the drawstring around the packs. I gave her an old t-shirt and voila, her stomach stuck out further than her tits.

"Now you look like a mainstream American," I said.

"That's mean."

"No, it's the sad truth," I said. "Two-thirds of your fellow Americans are overweight or obese, to say nothing of the morbidly obese."

She took a selfie of us in the mirror. We laughed and laughed. We were perfect—a skinny legged old fart and a dowdy old frump.

Getting in the car, she said, "Ugh, I don't see how they live like this."

We got on the interstate northbound. The radio was tuned to the Austin NPR station. Pretty soon we were out of range and I began scanning the dial. We were in the land of right-wing fundamentalist propaganda. We rode along alternately outraged and amused as the public airwaves spewed unrelenting, Christian-themed hatred and lies. We were really in the mainstream now. We stopped in Temple for lunch. We fit right in.

We continued north and exited at Jewell. Ava pulled out a small camera. I cruised slowly past the bank, which was really nothing to look at. It was maybe a little bigger than my house, maybe about the size of Beatriz's place, say about three or four thousand square feet. The place looked abandoned.

"I want to see inside," Ava said.

"It's Sunday," I said.

"Oh crap, you're right," she said.

"Anyway, how complicated could it be?" I said.

I circled around under the overpass and pulled up to the gas pumps. I put some gas in the van. Ava went inside to buy a bottle of water. I stood there scoping out the bank, which was right there in the same parking lot. It was sort of a portable or prefab building looked like if you had a three-quarter ton pickup you could hook a chain to it and drag it away.

We drove in silence for a ways.

"This is real," she said.

"You're right," I said.

Someplace south of Temple she said she had to pee. I whipped off the freeway, turned down a little dirt road and found a likely looking place.

"This'll do," I said. I stepped out, whipped out my piece and let fly. I got back in the van but she was just sitting there. "I thought you had to go," I said.

"I can't go here," she said.

"Sure you can," I said. "I just did."

"But I'm a girl," she said.

"Yeah, I know," I said, and gave her thigh a little squeeze.

She kept sitting there.

"Better hurry before someone comes along," I said.

She got out, dropped her drawers and took a squat inside the open door. She kept her eyes fixed on me the whole time. I gave her a big smile. She finished up and we got back on the highway.

"What was that?" she said.

"That was real," I said. "From now on, it's all real."

Back at my place, we changed back to our regular selves. She looked 20 years younger. "I don't think I'd like to be with that other woman," I said.

"I wouldn't want to be her," she said.

I ordered in a nice seafood pasta and chilled a bottle of sauvignon blanc. She was pretty quiet while we ate. While I was washing the plates she started gathering her stuff.

"Stay with me tonight," I said.

"I've got a lot more planning to do," she said.

"You're not ready for this," I said.

"I know, I've got to cast the scene, create the shot list..."

"Hold on," I said. I sat her down on the couch and perched on the coffee table in front of her. "You're not ready for this. I thought you had figured that out for yourself, once you saw how it was."

"I want to do this," she said. "I can do this."

"You can't do it like this."

"Like what?"

"Like you didn't even know what day it was. Then you got all emotional. If you're going to do this you've got to be totally self-conscious and unconscious at the same time. You've got to be zeroed in on the zone. You've got to have that total freedom and total control you feel sometimes playing sports or music or—or making love. It's a combination of highly developed skill, super intense focus and complete relaxation."

She wouldn't meet my eye. I took both her hands in mine.

"And then, when we stopped to pee. That was a reality check, too. You've got to be utterly ruthless, especially with yourself. You can't let any little barrier of social niceties make you hesitate even for an instant. You've got to move like lightning or freeze in mid-motion. You can't waste any time. You can't call any attention to yourself. You can't feel your emotions."

I took her face gently in my hands and turned her toward me.

"Honey," I said, "I'm telling you this for your own good." For sure that wasn't the right thing to say. Her eyes were burning. I kissed her hands. "I'm sorry," I said, "you're just not ready."

She couldn't hold my glance for long. "Well, how can I get ready?" she said.

"You need to get some experience."

She thought about that for a minute before a smile spread across her face. She stayed the night.

24

Geoff and I spent quite a bit of time on overdubbing till we had 21 fairly presentable songs on tape; we put the best 14 on the album. We felt pretty good about it, and it started leading to gigs right away.

Ava and I took a few day trips to the Hill Country, just looking around.

A couple of weeks went by before Beatriz texted and wanted to meet at her office. I was wondering how long it would take her.

She was dressed in a pants suit but nothing could hide those curves. She took her place behind the desk. The way she was acting all professional was kind of funny and sexy.

She was trying to hide the molten pools in her eyes. I knew exactly what she wanted. I gave her a warm, inviting smile. She looked down at her desk, then back at me.

"My client would like to meet with you," she said.

"I'm not in that line of work any more," I said.

"My client is worried that perhaps you have been offended," she said.

"If I was, you'd know."

"Then, why?"

"I came to my senses."

"He would like to talk to you directly," she said. "He was quite emphatic."

I was still smiling. "I don't think so."

"He has a new project he'd like to interest you in. Something more ambitious. More along the lines of project director."

I just smiled. "I work alone."

"Alex, please," she said. "This is not exactly how he put it, but there's always the possibility that, if you won't meet with him, he may become offended."

So that's how it was. "I'm not going to his place."

"When and where, all that can be negotiated."

"Someplace public. Someplace with lots of people but a little privacy. I don't want to be seen with him."

"I can work on that," she said.

"Is that all?" I said.

She looked like she was on the verge of tears. I got up to leave.

She stood. "Have you forgotten me so soon?"

I turned back to her. "I haven't forgotten."

She came around the desk. "So you've simply grown tired of me?"

In the next instant, she was in my arms. I had a lot of fun taking off that business suit, with all the frills and underthings. Then I had her up on the desk and she was laughing and crying at the same time. After that she took me back to her room and kept me in bed for the rest of the afternoon. She really knew how to get what she wanted.

I flopped over on my back, breathing hard. She curled up next to me and clung to me like a little girl.

"I love you," she whispered. She looked up at me hopefully.

I patted her fanny and gave her a smile.

25

One day Ava and I drove to Enchanted Rock in the morning and looked around, then pulled into Fredericksburg about lunch time. It's a pretty touristy place so we strolled up one side of the main street and down the other, like any other tourists, but there wasn't much to see and it was all pretty cheap. We went into the most expensive restaurant we saw—it sucked. But as we were leaving town, headed east toward Austin, I noticed something likely looking—a tidy little limestone bank with easy access to the highway. About a half a mile down the road around an easy curve was the everything store with its vast acreage of parking. I pulled in.

Ava said, "Why are we stopping here?" She knew I hated the place.

"I might have found something," I said.

I drove back past the little bank. "I like it," I said. "Kind of cute, don't you think?"

I turned around and headed east again. The speed limit changed from 45 to 55 just beyond the bank. In another minute we were beyond the city limits and cruising at 70. "This could work," I said. "What do you think?"

"You're the expert," she said.

The next day I rented a pickup and we wore cowboy hats and drove back to Fredericksburg. We drove every street, highway and back road on the north and west sides of town. The next day we came back and did the same on the south and east sides, checking and double-checking everything on the map.

We went to a gun show in San Antonio. In Texas, if you buy a gun from a private individual rather than a dealer there's no background check and no reporting of the sale. I bought her a cute little lady's revolver, and I decided to pick up a big black 9 mm auto for more of a visual intimidation factor, along with a holster I could clip on my belt in the small of my back. I took her to a funky old range out in the country, and after a few hundred rounds she was hitting what she aimed at.

I looked around and found a guy who sold me a car without a title. It's not illegal—guys do it all the time for a vehicle to use on the ranch or the deer lease, just not on the public thoroughfare. But this guy looked pretty sketchy; he had to know that's not what I wanted it for.

The exterior was rough—urban camouflage of rusty black and primer gray, with a mismatched passenger door, missing chrome, and no back bumper. The interior was shot. But the tires were good, the suspension was solid, and under the hood was a big V8. I gave eight hundred for it.

I wasn't taking this thing anywhere near my place, or Ava's. I called her and had me meet her in the gigantic parking lot of a 24-hour super center in South Austin—far beyond the hipster nightspots, boutiques and coffee shops, into honest to god mainstream America.

I gave her the quadrant to park in and spotted her after a couple of passes. I found a space where there were a lot of cars and parked. I went inside and bought a bottle of water, so I was a customer, then walked back to her car. I surprised her when I tapped on the window.

"Hi baby," I said. "Let's go. We've got a lot to do and an early start in the morning."

We cruised slowly by the car to give her a good look so she could imagine what kind of people would drive it.

"We're going in that?" she said.

"It's better than it looks," I said.

"We'll be meth heads," she said.

"Good," I said. "But I don't want anything that can slip up or fall off or go wrong in a critical moment, all right? Nothing fancy, nothing complicated, nothing that can get in our way. And we need to be able to quickly shift our look."

She dropped me at a car rental agency while she went to a thrift store. I rented a mid-size sedan, which turned out to be a silver Toyota. Perfect. She met me at my place. For me, she had a denim shirt that had seen better days. She sprinkled and smudged some paint on it, and rubbed some grime from the underside of her car on it too, then further distressed the already fraying hems and seams and added a couple of nice holes. Underneath I'd wear a silk t-shit and clean jeans. My running shoes were fairly well worn, so they'd do fine. We'd leave a light blazer on the back seat of the rental. For herself she picked a faded red hoody. She cut the arms out and sprinkled it with paint and smeared on some of the grime. Underneath she would have a tank top, jeans and tennis shoes, and like me would leave behind a light cover up.

The next morning we were up before light. She gave me bleached blonde hair with black roots, a few meth sores on my face and prison tattoos on my forearms. She gave herself some meth sores and a rebel flag tattoo on her left shoulder. She was really good at wardrobe and makeup—all those years of experience in film. I wondered how many.

She pulled out a couple of mini-cams. "No," I said. "I don't want you distracted."

"But I want to study the tapes," she said.

"No," I said.

"But how else can I learn?"

Finally I relented. I could never say no to her.

As we were going out, I thought to cover my hair with that Longhorn cap in case one of my neighbors was up early.

It was getting light by the time we got to South Austin. The parking lot was fairly full, and the four-door was waiting faithfully where I left it. As I was getting out of the car, I reminded her, "We're not in any hurry. We don't want to be there before 9:30. Just take it easy and enjoy the ride."

She gave me a tight little smile. I leaned over and tried to kiss her. "No," she said, "you're gross."

"Kiss me," I said. She gave me a quick peck.

She took off. I got in the other car, shifted to another parking lot and waited. I wanted to give her a good head start. I wanted her waiting for me when I pulled up in this rig. I didn't want to wait for her.

I tooled out into the Hill Country. It was a beautiful morning, a Wednesday. Nothing ever happens on a Wednesday.

I stopped once and pulled off on a little dirt road to pee. I told her to do the same thing when she got to the location.

I pulled into the parking lot and drove up toward the front. She came out of the store right on cue, hood up, hands in her pockets and kind of shuffling but making pretty good time. She looked like a meth head. She was carrying a couple of tote bags with the store's logo.

She got in the car. Her eyes were big. "Everything's going to be cool," I said. "If you tunnel, if you get confused, if you forget what you're doing or lose focus, look to me."

She pointed to my head. I still had the cap on. I took it off and threw it in the back.

We drove the few seconds to the bank and pulled up in front. There were about five cars in the parking lot. I parked as close as I could. We went inside. Out came the weapons. I disarmed the guard and she covered the two tellers and three patrons. I walked straight to the manager and showed him the gun. He was a tall, bald, soft-looking mainstream American about 45. He looked scared but remained calm.

"I want the big denominations," I said, "and no dye-packs." He led me to the vault and put what looked like five or six thousand in the bags. I made him riffle through each stack and show me it was clean.

We went back into the lobby. Ava was keeping it together. The guard, another fat guy, was looking pretty pissed off. "Don't even think about it, dipshit," I said, and let him get a good look at the gun.

We slipped outside, hopped in the car and roared onto the highway. I put on the cap. Seconds later we were shifting to the rental. We drove around behind the store to the car wash. I whipped off the denim shirt and she pulled her hoodie over her head. She went to work on me with wet wipes and took off my tattoos and sores, then removed her own with a couple of swipes. I dumped the old clothes in the trash and we put on our jackets. I pulled slowly out of the parking lot and turned toward town.

"What are you doing?" she said.

"It's an old trick," I said, "but maybe they haven't heard of it."

When we passed the bank, there were already two police cars in the parking lot, and another one passed us at high speed heading east. We cruised through town and turned north toward Enchanted Rock, like any other tourists.

"That was fun," she said.

"You did fine," I said.

"Funny, I didn't get scared until after."

"Good."

"How much did we get?" she said.

"What difference does it make?" I said.

We had barbecue in Llano and came home by a different route.

We unpacked, cleaned up, dropped off the rental and were finished in time to catch ourselves on the six o'clock news. They had some grainy security footage—we looked like a couple of meth heads. They hadn't found the car. We had a good laugh about that.

"So what did you learn?" I said.

"I don't know," she said. "It all went by so fast."

We reviewed some of the footage. "Wow," she said. "It's different than it seems."

"Yeah," I said.

She insisted on counting the money. It came to a little over $5,000.

"Not too bad," she said.

"Not as good as you think," I said. "We spent like eight hundred on the car. The rentals cost us a couple hundred. We spent two full days researching and planning."

"Still."

"It's going to take you a long time to make a million at this rate."

"I see what you're saying," she said. "It would have to be an act of desperation."

"Yeah."

She looked out the window. "I've got some rewriting to do," she said.

She came over and sat next to me on the couch.

"So, do you think I'm ready?" she said. She looked doubtful.

"No," I said. "I don't think so. Let's try it again, and give you a little more to do this time."

26

I sent Ava scouting to the east. In the meantime, I got back to my workout routine. I was biking or swimming two, three hours a day. I was playing guitar every day an hour or two, and reading about the same. I was eating well and going easy on the booze.

I took a cup of coffee to the garden and visited the cats. They were swarming all over me—except for this new little seal point. I hadn't seen her before. She was the prettiest little thing. She hung back behind the other cats and wouldn't come when I called her. I tried to pet her but she scampered away. Then she stretched out on the gravel walkway. I approached her very slowly and slowly extended my hand to give her a gentle pet, and she flipped over on her back and bared her claws and fangs. Later she caught a katydid and played with it like a favorite toy, then casually dismembered it and ate the good parts.

Three days later Ava called and came over. She had found something, maybe, she said. We drove out to Bastrop to check it out. I didn't quite care for the layout. So I sent her north. A few days later, she reported back. She had found something in Round Rock. "A little close to home, don't you think?" I said. "Anyway, those people are too sophisticated—and too mean."

I could see she was tired. She needed a break.

"Hey, let's go to the beach," I said.

We drove down to Port Aransas and got a condo on the water. We took long walks on the beach mornings and evenings, and during the heat of the day we drove all over the area. Corpus Christi was too urban. Kingsville was like one way in one way out. On the third day we found a little bank in Rockport I liked the look of. We looked around till we found a wildlife viewing area on the Goliad highway where you could park and walk on some hiking trails. Then we went back to the beach.

The next day we came home. She got to work on our characters. I would be oil field trash in coveralls and a brightly colored welder's cap. Underneath would be shorts and a tank top. She would be a biker chick in blue jeans and a blue jean jacket with her hair under a scarf. Under that she would wear a one-piece bathing suit with shorts and a t-shirt over it. She bought a pair of faded jeans at the thrift shop that were too big for her; the extra layers would make her look kind of fat.

I rented another sedan, a silver Ford this time. "Won't we need another car?" she said.

"Yeah," I said, "we'll pick up something down there."

We went back to the beach. The next day we drove into Corpus looking for a likely vehicle. We looked around for a while till I had second thoughts. "You know," I said, "I don't want to drive a hot car that far."

We drove over to Rockport. There was a big grocery store just a couple of blocks from the bank. We sat in the parking lot till a dark gray SUV pulled up and a fat woman with four fat kids got out. "They'll be in there for a while," I said.

I jumped out and Ava got behind the wheel. "See you in a few," I said.

She took off. I jacked the truck and followed her to the drop point. We pulled into the parking lot. We were the only people there. We slid into our costumes. She gave me some very realistic looking salt-and-pepper stubble and a soul patch. She gave herself a big teardrop tattoo under her left eye. Anyone looking at her face, that's what they'd remember.

All this had taken about 15 minutes. I figured the car was still cool, but not by much. We drove back to the bank and parked right in front. We went inside. She took the lead. The guard was clear across the room. She threw down on him and ordered him to give up his weapon. When he hesitated, then started fumbling at his holster, she crossed the room in three strides and smashed him right in the mouth with her pistol. He groaned and went down. She bashed him on the head and he was out. Everyone was astonished, including me.

The manager came out of a back office. "What's going on?" he said.

She stuck that pistol right under his double chin and said, "Make it large denominations and no dye packs." He nearly shit.

While they were in the vault I had the easy job of covering the tellers and a few customers. I secured the guard's weapon so he wouldn't come to and fuck up. "Don't worry," I said. "Everybody just take it easy, and we'll be gone before you know it."

She came out of the vault following the manager, just like I'd told her. Then we were out of there. Back at the park, a family were gathered around their car putting on sunscreen and bug spray.

"Oh shit," Ava said.

"We're cool," I said.

We pulled in, got out of the truck and walked back into the woods. As soon as we were out of sight we shucked our disguises and ditched them, then turned around and came out of the woods, just another couple of tourists. The family were still there. They didn't give us a second look. We got in the rental and drove north a ways, then turned left and cut over to the freeway, then turned left again and went back to our condo on the beach.

Ava counted the money. We'd only taken about three thousand this time.

"This is no way to make a living," she said.

"You did good back there," I said.

"Thanks," she said.

"You kind of surprised me."

"What, doing good?"

"No, the way you beat the shit out of that guy."

"He was stupid."

"No shit."

"He should have done what he was told."

"He probably thought, because you're a woman, you know…"

"He was a fool," she said. "Did you see how fat he was?"

"Probably the only job he could get."

We went to this little place right on the fishing docks and had Gulf shrimp and blue crab and plenty of cold beer.

We went to bed and she fell right to sleep. I've never needed much sleep. I studied the lines of her face. She looked so innocent and peaceful. I felt restless. I got up and went for a long walk on the beach under the stars. I walked right along the swash-line. The waves advanced and retreated. An old-looking moon rose, throwing a long arm of light across the water. I walked a long time till I came to a jetty made of huge chunks of granite that jutted way out to sea. I stood there taking it all in, feeling something, I don't know what, something powerful, something awesome, something infinitely creative and infinitely sad. Something brushed against my leg and startled me. It was a cat, a gaunt, orange cat. He mewed at me and rubbed against my leg.

"What are you doing here?" I said.

He looked toward the jetty. I followed his gaze. The rocks were swarming with cats. They leapt and surged and poured among the boulders—a regular colony. The waves hissed on the sand. The moon pulled on the ocean. The stars, in their vast indifference, went their own way. Down here, it was just me and the cats.

The next morning we drove home like any other couple.

"Well, what do you think?" I said.

"About what?" she said.

"I think you're ready," I said.

She gave me a big smile.

27

By the time we got home, unpacked, cleaned up and dropped off the rental, I was beat.

"Do you want to review the footage?" she said.

"Nah, I don't think so," I said.

She went to leave, and I didn't try to stop her.

I poured a nice tumbler of Scotch and took it out to the garden. It was high summer so there were a couple of hours of daylight left. The cats were sleeping in the shade. It was hot but the air was kind of dry and it felt good to just sit there and bake in the heat. One jaybird was crying ever once in a while. A tiny bit of breeze tickled the leaves of the desert willow. This is the kind of moment when you can truly appreciate the peace and quiet of my little neighborhood.

It felt so good to just let go and not have to think about anything and worry about everything and go, go, go and do, do, do. I had been busy lately, I realized. Well, it was better than being bored.

I lifted my glass and saw that it was empty. Not that I needed it, but I went inside and poured a couple more fingers. I went out and settled into my chair. The lop-eared cat stretched with infinite, unconscious grace, lightly hopped into the other chair, curled up and went back to sleep. Cats can sleep 20 hours a day—they really have the right idea.

The angle of the light was throwing longer shadows. The sun was balancing on the neighbor's trees. The color of the air was rich and gold.

The cats started circling, wary of each other but wanting something from me. Seemed like there were several new cats I'd never seen. The little seal point kept her distance but she was watching me closely. She was the prettiest thing. Her body was a light cream, her tail and feet a deep chocolate brown, her face and ears almost black, and she had the prettiest blue eyes you ever saw. She kept watching me with those pale blue eyes in that deep black face. It was almost unnatural how blue her eyes were, like she could look right into me and tell what I was thinking.

A dove was mourning like he'd lost his one true love. The others echoed his cries, matching his rhythm in call and response. The cicadas clicked on their preternatural, penetrating drone. A neighbor walked by on the street with a little dog on a leash. The cats and I froze. Neither dog nor neighbor noticed us.

The little seal point was peering intently into a dense tangle of esperanza and mountain laurel. Invisibly, she leapt. There was a fluttering and flapping screened by the leaves. The cats came to attention. The dove were doing their call and response. The cicadas passed their mindless, alien chant from tree to tree like fire from torch to torch. The mosquitos came out of hiding and started to whine. The little cat emerged from the leaves with a dead dove in her mouth to the silent applause of the other cats. They made a lane for her. She ceremoniously paced as if for a processional and presented me her kill. She laid the lifeless body at my feet and gazed upward with those ghostly blue eyes.

"Thanks," I said. She paraded proudly around the circle of cats, her tail straight in the air, the tip twitching from side to side.

I stood. The little cat scampered. I started for the door. Lop-ear appropriated the dove and start taking it apart. The little cat darted into the door ahead of me.

"Hey, wait a minute," I said.

She made a mad dash for the studio. I tried to catch her. She hid behind the drums. When I edged around the cymbals she leapt on an amplifier and then onto the high window ledge. I approached and she hopped lightly onto the keyboard and in two bounds was out the door. I ran after her into the living room. She cleverly evaded me with cunning use of cover, agile dodging and well-timed sprints. I followed her from room to room as she explored and assessed. I felt stupid and clumsy and more and more angry.

I finally cornered her in the laundry room. I was grabbing for her when she sprang to the top of the water heater and spotted a place where a panel was kind of loose and climbed right up into the ceiling. I started pulling down the ceiling and broken tiles and dust and insulation were raining down on my head just in time to see the cat fly down the crawl space and drop between the studs of an interior wall. I kind of collapsed against the dryer and slid down into a sitting position amid the rubble. I looked at the ruins and thought about all the time and energy it would take to repair the ceiling and clean up this mess and suddenly started crying.

I know it sounds stupid and pathetic but I sat there and sobbed and wept and blubbered and bawled till I could barely breathe. I didn't even know why. When I could catch my breath I went to the bathroom and washed my face and blew my nose and you would never believe that much mucous could come out of a person's face.

I felt sick and exhausted. I went to bed without taking off my clothes. The little cat was crying through the walls. The cats outside were yowling in reply. I covered my head with my pillow. The night birds croaked and groaned. The mosquitos' persistent whine penetrated the windows as they bumped and fumbled and groped for a way in. They were trying to drag me down to the place they were all heading for.

The weeping and groaning and whining and groping were all aimed at the same thing—me. I stuck my fingers in my ears and keened and moaned to shut it all out. I shivered and trembled and struggled to breathe. I could see a body from a distance alive with maggots and flies, my body.

I must have fallen asleep because when I woke I had wet the bed. I stripped off my clothes and stripped the sheets and put them in the washer. I felt like a total freak when I saw the mess in the laundry room. Somewhere far away I could hear something weeping in a tiny little voice of someone lost and far away.

I put a towel on the wet place on the mattress and wrapped myself in my comforter as tight as I could, including my head; only my feet were sticking out. I lay there a long time, alone and sick and afraid.

I lay there I don't know how long until I had to pee so bad I couldn't hold it any longer and I didn't want to wet myself again like some miserable, pathetic loser. I struggled out of the swaddling blanket and barely made it to the bathroom before bursting. I stood there kind of shaking and gasping; the release felt so good it hurt. I was almost in tears. I started to the kitchen to get a drink of water and saw the little seal point sitting all prim and proper beside the door with those bright blue eyes fixed on me. I opened the door and she stepped primly over the threshold. I went to the kitchen, and there in the middle of the floor she had left a neat little pile of shit full of bug parts and bird feathers. It was almost more than I could handle. I couldn't find the dust pan and I started crying again when I was trying to pick it up with a paper towel and I got it all over my hand and I ran outside and threw it at the cats but they weren't there, and a neighbor was walking her dog and I realized I was naked and I ran back inside and smeared cat shit on the door handle. I was heaving huge breaths trying to regain control and I settled down a little and stumbled to the sink and washed my hands and washed my face and blew out long streams of gelatinous nastiness from my nose and hacked up huge gobs of gunk from my lungs. I staggered to the toilet and threw up and threw up and threw up but there was nothing to throw up.

I went to bed. I buried my head in pillows and wrapped myself in my blanket and was never going to get out of bed. I wrapped myself so tight I couldn't move. My weight was too heavy to float. I sank 30 or 40 or 100 feet below the muddy water until all I could see of the sun was a distant, murky glow.

The phone rang from time to time. At length the horror and sickness and fear receded and I wallowed in doubt and shame. What was I doing? Why was I doing it? How did it come to this? I wished I had Ava with me, or Beatriz, but I couldn't stand the thought of facing anyone.

"What is happening?" I wondered. I didn't need to wonder. I knew.

It had never gone this far. I had never let it go this far. I have always managed to take control, put on a happy face and count my blessings, accomplishments and goals, lose myself in turning to new tasks. Be strong, be Mama's little man, you weakling, you unwanted baby. I struggled to get up but the blankets were too tight and it was darker than ever. Then I must have slept for a long, long time because when I woke up I was as tired and sore as if I'd run a marathon. I was dying of thirst. I got a drink, squeezed out a tiny trickle of urine and went back to bed. I must have slept a long time because when I saw the morning light it had been four days since I'd left the house.

Everyone had called me, but I didn't feel like talking to anyone. I didn't have the energy. I felt like I'd gone on a long trek in the wilderness or suffered a serious illness. I was coming back, but I was tired.

I heated a can of chicken broth and drank that. I lay on the couch wrapped in my blanket and felt a thin stream of nourishment trickling through my body. That made me hungry. I cooked a soft-boiled egg and ate it carefully. At first, I didn't think I would keep it down, but then my stomach went to work and I lay back on the couch and nearly passed out. Later I made a cup of coffee and put in a lot of milk and sugar. That started to perk me up.

Then I remembered—then and only then. I felt like an idiot, forgetting Psychopharmacology 101. How does a person do that? I went to the medicine cabinet and saw I had two ounces and maybe a quarter left. Where had it all gone? Oh well, after this little boost, just a little starter fluid, really, I told myself I would lay off.

28

I called Geoff first. I figured that would be easiest.

"Hey man, how's it going?" he said.

"Okay," I said. "I wasn't feeling too good for a couple of days there. I must have let my phone die."

"I had to pass on a gig because I couldn't get in touch with you."

"Sorry, man. Next time, you know, just go without me."

"I don't want to do that, man, you're the soul of the band."

"Naw, man, that'd be you."

"No, I'm the heart, the brains maybe, but you're the soul."

"Well, thanks man."

"I love you, brother. Anyway, I've got some gigs lined up."

"Send me the details and I'll put them in my calendar."

"Will do."

"Think we need to rehearse?"

"Nah, I think we're good, don't you?"

"Yeah, probably."

"Okay, see you Saturday then," he said.

"Cool, okay, see you then.

I called Ava. No answer. For someone I wanted to spend the rest of my life with, she was getting to be damned hard to communicate with.

I called Beatriz. She wanted to meet, of course. I figured I could handle this. I figured she should be getting the idea by now.

I showered and got dressed. I was looking good, but I was feeling kind of rocky. I snorted a couple of lines just to make sure.

She was dressed modestly, in black slacks and a sleeveless blouse, but no matter how she was dressed, when I looked at her all I could think of was one thing.

She seemed shy. She gave me the name of the place where I was to meet Johnson—one of the fancier Mexican restaurants in town—and a date, September 16.

I checked my calendar. "Okay," I said. "Anything else?"

"Yes," she said, looking me full in the eye. "I'm pregnant."

Unless you've been there, you have no idea how many thoughts go flying through a man's head at a time like this. The most obvious—how do you know it's mine?—it's better not to say aloud.

I stood up, stepped around the desk, took her hand, led her to the bedroom and made sweet, tender, passionate love to her. She was smiling through her tears.

I fell back on the bed exhausted. She curled up next to me and put her head on my shoulder and wrapped my arm around her and held on tight. "Oh baby," she said, "I love you. You don't know how much I love you."

My other arm was trapped under her. I petted her shoulder, which was the only thing I could reach.

"Do you still love me," she said.

"You know how I feel about you," I said.

"What do you want to do?" she said.

"I don't know," I said. "I'm trying to think."

"We could make it, baby," she said. "I love you so much I want to spend my whole life with you just loving you and taking care of you and having your babies."

"That could be damned awkward," I said, "given who you work for."

"We could move out of state," she said.

We lay there for a while.

"Look," I said, "we could just, you know, and it would all be simple and we could go along like we have been."

"Doesn't it mean anything to you?"

"Yes, of course, but I only want you."

"Well, anyway, I'm Catholic."

"So am I. So what?"

"It goes against my faith."

"Are you going to listen to a bunch of old fags in Rome, or are you going to do what I say?"

"And you'll love me then?"

"I already do."

We lay there a while longer.

"Baby?" she said.

"Let me think," I said.

"Don't take too long," she said. "I'll start to show soon."

She had this dreamy smile on her face, like that was exactly what she wanted. There was something triumphant about it, and something of a threat. She was starting to piss me off.

29

I went home and tried to think.

I paced around the house. I toyed with the drums. I went outside and paced around the garden. I tried to think about Beatriz, but I kept thinking about Ava. I needed to give her a call, but I didn't know what to say to her.

I went to bed and covered up my head but all I could hear was a dull thud like plodding feet and the dead clank of an iron bell.

I couldn't lie still so I got up and went out to sit with the cats. I could still hear the bell clanking. Maybe it was a church, or construction. My neighborhood is usually so quiet.

The crepuscular hour was coming on. The cats ignored me and went about their business, all except the little seal point who lay in the other chair and stared at me with her cool blue eyes.

I thought about Ava, and I thought about Beatriz. I couldn't get beyond their first names. Ava, Beatriz, Beatriz, Ava.

I have always prided myself on my rationality, my ability to think things through. I like to understand the circumstances, know the lay of the land, know the players and plan ahead to stay in control. I like to think I know myself pretty well. I know what I'm thinking and feeling and I know why. But I didn't know if I was angry or scared.

The dove were cooing like crazy. The cat continued to stare at me. "What do you want?" I said.

"Meow," she said.

I went inside. I realized my hands were balled up in fists and my jaw was so tight it hurt. Time to self-medicate. I pulled out a fat nugget of California marijuana. I loaded up a pipe and stoked it standing right there in the kitchen. When I finished one bowl I burned another. I went into the living room, lay back in my chair, put my feet up and closed my eyes.

Marijuana, like any psycho-active substance, affects different people in different ways. Some it confuses, some become paranoid, some get stupid, some get hungry. I have always found it calming yet stimulating, calming to the body and stimulating to the mind. For me, it is the herb of contemplation.

The phone rang. It was Ava. I'd have to call her back later.

I thought about Beatriz and I thought about Ava. I thought about Ava and I thought about Beatriz. Literally, when I was thinking about Beatriz I'd be thinking about Ava, and vice versa.

A lot of the time what I was thinking wasn't thinking at all but raw images and scarcely pent-up instincts. My dick got hard.

Ava was the one I loved, obviously, but in toying with Beatriz I had let myself develop some sort of feelings for her. Ava I wanted to spend the rest of my life with. She could be self-willed and self-absorbed, she could be hard to communicate with sometimes, but she was sexy, intelligent, artistic—hell, I admired her. We had so much going on we were like a partnership already. We had so much invested in each other, not so much money, though there was that, but trust. We were in a position where we absolutely had to trust each other absolutely.

Beatriz, on the other hand, what did she have going on? Was she really an attorney, or just a high-priced whore? She was a hell of a woman, that was sure, but did she even have a mind? Her feelings were evident. Or were they? I hadn't stopped to think about what she might be thinking or even if she was thinking. She couldn't be that dumb; she had to have some kind of smarts for Johnson to employ her for this kind of job. What kind of job was it? Simply liaison, or was she keeping tabs on me? Why would Johnson want to keep tabs on me. Why wouldn't he? What would he say or do when he learned she was pregnant with my child. Was she really pregnant with my child? Was she really pregnant? I had no proof. I realized I had stupidly simply taken her word. That was it. I would demand proof. Get tough with her. Freeze her out, even as I met my responsibilities to the kid if she insisted on having it. Get some kind of sealed court order. That would be expensive, but—but it would mean she would be out of my life and never—never again would I be bothered by—never again would I—would I touch her abundant body and feel her astonishing, overwhelming mind-altering passion and, I had to admit it, her generous, sympathetic, loving heart. She pissed me off sometimes, but I couldn't help loving her a little.

But Ava was the one, after all. She was good in bed, too. I wondered how old she was. I would have to ask. I had been able to open up to her in ways I never had with anyone before, except my mother. I had shared with her parts of my life that I had never shared before. I really felt she knew me. But her knowledge could be a dangerous thing, if she had a change of feeling. Beatriz, I realized belatedly, knew a lot about me too, and her knowledge, too, could be dangerous, whatever her feeling.

Finally I gave up and went to bed. I lay the whole night between sleeping and waking. I'm not sure I could tell the difference anymore. I lay perfectly still for like twelve hours while behind my eyelids unreeled a hundred lucid dreams, most of them ending in sex or death.

In some of the thousand and one scenarios I entertained, Beatriz would simply pass away and my problem would disappear. But Beatriz was young and apparently quite healthy, necessitating an awful intervention of violence. I abhor violence, of course, but sometimes a highly judicious and precisely targeted use of violence is the only reasonable course. She lived in the hills—a crash involving faulty brakes could be deadly. But then again she could survive, scarred or maimed. A burglar could confront her with a gun, quick and clean, more or less. But any burglar, especially if he were me, would first feel compelled to sample her conspicuous charms, especially if she were scantily clad in one of her revealing nighties. And then he would be hooked on her line, ensnared in her web and held by her gravity. For what heterosexual male could bring himself to contemplate the destruction of that beautiful body?

I may have slept a little toward dawn. I rose refreshed. I made a cup of coffee and went outside. I could feel the heat coming, somewhere over the horizon. The cats seemed like they were glad to see me, but they probably just wanted something. Still, on this morning, I could enjoy their aloof and independent companionship.

After all, why did I have to make all the decisions? Maybe my need to be in control made me too controlling. Maybe I should just take things as they come, play it by ear, at least for the time being. How bad could it be?

I went inside to call Ava but it was like 6:30. I went to the studio and started playing my D-28, since I didn't want to disturb the neighbors. Acoustic guitar is a totally different instrument from electric. The electric has all that power and sustain, and you're playing the amp as much as the guitar. The acoustic is just a wooden box with a few wires stretched across it; you have to stroke it and spank it, caress it and thump it and breathe life into it to awaken the life in it. In this way it's exactly like making love to a woman. With that thought I instantly was distracted and couldn't play for thinking of one specific part of Beatriz's anatomy.

I went into the kitchen. Only an hour had passed. I decided I should eat. How long had it been since I had eaten? I couldn't remember.

I slow-cooked a batch of hash browns, baked scratch biscuits and whipped up some cream gravy, then fried some bacon and a couple of eggs in my cast iron skillet. Breakfast is all about timing. Everything was ready at the same time and I sat down with a real sense of satisfaction at a job well done, but I couldn't eat half of it.

At last it was time to call Ava. I called. No answer.

Now I was pissed. I decided to go swimming. How long had it been since I'd had a proper workout. I couldn't even remember. I could barely go a half a mile and I felt like puking. I lay in the grass and fell asleep and woke up with a touch of sunburn. I plunged in the cool water, dried off and drove home.

I tried Ava again. Again no answer. Now I felt totally justified in having not returned her calls. I mean, if she was going to do me this way I might as well do her that way, right?

She finally called about five. "Hey," I said.

"Hey," she said.

"Where've you been?" I said.

"My phone died," she said.

"Ha, mine too," I said. "I tried to call."

"Yeah, I saw, today. I never heard it ring. But I've been trying to call you all week."

"Why didn't you come by?"

"I did."

"Hmm. Maybe I was out."

"Your car was there."

"Maybe I was asleep."

"It was the middle of the day."

"I wasn't feeling so good there for a couple of days."

"I knocked. I rang the bell."

"Sorry I missed you."

"No, I'm sorry you were sick. What was the matter?"

"I don't know. Maybe something I ate."

"Did you go to the doctor?"

"Nothing the doctor could do, probably."

"I wish you had called. I would have made you some chicken soup."

I laughed. "That's sweet," I said.

"How are you feeling now?"

"Okay."

"We need to talk," she said.

The four words every man dreads. "Okay," I said. "What about?"

"The movie. You know. The scene."

"What scene?"

"You know. The scene."

"What about it?"

"I don't want to go into it on the phone."

"Okay. When and where?"

"Wouldn't you like to come over?" She sounded wistful. I had her where I wanted her.

"Yeah. Okay. When?"

"As soon as, you know, you can. I can fix you some enchiladas."

"I'll be there in about an hour," I said.

"Okay," she said.

30

I had to stall around but I made it a point to arrive at Ava's an hour and a half later. I made sure to bring some money.

As soon as I was in the door I took her in my arms and kissed her. She seemed a little tentative. I sat down on the couch and patted the cushion beside me. She perched on the edge of the chair across the coffee table. She kind of leaned in and looked me over.

"Are you all right?" she said.

"Yeah," I said. "Why?"

"You seemed so distant on the phone."

"I did? I didn't mean to."

"Is something wrong?"

"No. Like what?"

"I don't know."

"I know what's wrong," I said. "Come here."

She came and sat beside me. I took her in my arms. I kissed her. I took her to bed. I don't like to kiss and tell, but I can tell you that what happened next was magical.

However, I was just postponing the inevitable. The timer buzzed. We got dressed and sat down to dinner. The enchiladas were fantastic. The wine was so-so.

"This is what we ate the first time we made love," I said.

"Yeah," she said. "So, we've got to talk about the scene. We've got to plan."

"I don't know why you keep calling it a scene when it's a robbery."

"It's going to be a scene in my movie."

"Like what do you mean?"

"Like a big scene. The biggest scene. The climax."

"That's insane."

"But that's what all this practice has been about, right? About getting it right so we can get it right. You know, when we, you know, hit those places and shoot the scene."

"I thought it was about you learning what it's like so you could, you know, stage it more realistically."

"No way. It has to be real. It can't be fake."

"Are you serious?"

"Of course!"

"Take it easy."

"This is important."

"I know. You can't put your face and my face in a movie while we're committing a robbery."

"You won't see us. We'll be behind the camera. You'll just see our hands and guns and stuff."

"Yeah but your camera will see me and mine will see you."

"I'll cut around it."

"It won't matter. They'll be able to tell. How are you even going to release it?"

"I'm not sure yet. I think I can alter it enough in post. Maybe blur the faces a little, maybe recreate some of the reactions."

"The people in the bank, you know, the victims? They'll be able to tell."

"They'll never even see a little indie film like this. And by that time, it'll have been noticed, and…"

"Yeah," I said.

"I said I think I can make it work. If not, I'll do something else."

"You once said I can't stop you from doing something stupid. I suppose that's right. But I can stop myself."

"Well, I don't want to, but if I have to I guess I can recast."

"Recast?"

"Yeah. You know, your role."

I laughed. "You're determined to make me a movie star, aren't you?

"Yes," she said.

"And you're going to go through with it, aren't you?"

"Yes."

"I can't let you do it alone."

"Oh baby!" She came around the table, sat in my lap and gave me a big kiss. "I love you," she said.

She gave me another kiss, a quick one. "We've got lot's of planning to do."

"Besides costumes, make-up, vehicles, the usual?"

"Yeah, we've got casting, a shot-list…"

"Casting?"

"Yeah, for the scene."

"You mean actors?"

"Yeah."

"Have you completely lost your mind?"

"I have some people in mind. We can trust them."

"I thought you said you can't trust actors."

"I meant, not with the script."

"Look, this is my life. Our lives. Our life together. I don't want to spend it in jail, without you."

"I'll just tell them I'm going for maximum realism. I'll tell them to stay in character and not talk to anyone on set."

"They'll believe that?"

"Yeah. Actors are stupid."

"I'm not taking any stupid people on this job."

"Not stupid. Gullible."

"I don't want to meet any of these people—not in connection with a crime."

"These people are professionals. They're artists."

"I don't care."

"But I need a crowd."

"We'll go the Tuesday after Labor Day. They'll be busy."

"I want my own people."

"I'm not going to commit a felony with a bunch of people I don't know."

"How many, then?"

"What do you mean?"

"If not a bunch, how about a few?"

"No, nor a couple nor anyone. I'm already breaking my own rule by taking you along."

We—she—finally settled on one, call him Ed. He was a comedian, she said, trying to take on more serious roles.

I still wasn't happy. "What about when he reads it in the newspaper or sees it on TV?"

"Ed doesn't read the newspaper, and he doesn't own a TV. If he hears anything, I'll just tell him it's part of the publicity. You know, creating buzz for the release."

"Do you need any money?" I said, trying to guilt-trip her.

"Alex, have you forgotten that we stole over $8,000 in the last two weeks?"

I shrugged. "Is that enough?"

"Yeah. I can't pay him too much. Then he would get suspicious."

I had a sudden thought. "What about the footage from the earlier jobs?" I said. "Have you erased it?

"I'm still studying it. Maybe we can use some of it," she said.

31

It took a lot of effort, but I was determined to stay in my laid back, take things as they come, whatever mode. I left the planning to Ava and I figured maybe I could get everything with her worked out pretty soon and the thing with Beatriz would more or less take care of itself.

One of Geoff's gigs came up, in Fredericksburg. Randy was with us so we were a five-piece, and with the gear there was only room for four in Geoff's little SUV. So I took my car. It was really nice to get out on the open road again; it had been too long. I lit up a fattie and listened to the Stones the whole way. I was feeling pretty good when I got to the gig, an outdoor beer garden. I had a beer sent up to the bandstand and it came in a plastic cup. That kind of place. I was in a cowboy shirt and torn up jeans. We started to play and in walked the manager of the bank on the highway—soft-looking, tall, 40 or 50 pounds overweight—definitely the same guy. I fucked up and hit the entirely wrong chord on a song I've played a hundred times and would have derailed the whole band if Randy hadn't covered for me. I had to drop out and pick it up again at the chorus. Geoff gave me a look like what the fuck. Nobody in the audience seemed to notice. They weren't paying attention to the music anyway. The bank manager sat down at a table in front with a bunch of people and a couple of pitchers and this wasn't his first beer. He started talking over the music and his friends were talking too and he started talking over them and they were all laughing and I could barely hear my own guitar. But I was playing through my clone Twin and that little buddy has got a pair—two 12-inch speakers pushed by 85 watts of pure electric mojo. I cranked up and raved but these people just talked louder so I cranked it again. This amp is so loud I rarely turn it above three and now I was at eight and it was howling like it was fixing to bust wide open. I was playing like a maniac. Geoff gave me a look. Everyone else had to turn up too of course. We rocked the house. The banker at last acknowledged us with a look of extreme distaste. He looked me over pretty good as the instigator. I was playing just for him and grinning in his face. He and his party got up and left. Hey fuck that guy. He didn't know shit.

After the gig, Geoff said, "Hey, man, what the fuck?"

"He was an asshole," I said.

"We don't want to run off the audience," he said.

"They weren't listening."

I thought about it on the drive home, about why I did that. I mean, he was disrespectful, but musicians get that all the time, playing in noisy clubs. So why did I have to confront him. I finally thought fuck it, it's rock and roll, and cranked up the Stones.

The next day was Saturday and we had a gig downtown that night. I went to Ava's in the afternoon to go over the plan. Ed was there. She introduced him as Ed. She introduced me as Jerry. He was a skinny guy with long hair and bad teeth. He had a kind of smell about him.

"Okay, see you Tuesday," he said.

Ava said, "Next Tuesday, not this Tuesday, next Tuesday."

"Oh, yeah, right," he said. He lit a cigarette. "Well, I don't want to miss the bus." He took off walking heroically in the high summer heat. I didn't like to dwell on it because it only made things worse, but Austin's heat was awesome. Nobody walked in this town. And who would ride the bus? We had the worst public transit in the world. Ed was wearing baggy shorts, white socks, beat-up tennis shoes and a canvas jungle hat. He looked ridiculous. He looked—I suddenly laughed—he looked like I did when we cased the joint.

"You sure he can handle it?" I said.

"Yeah. He'll be fine," she said.

"He looks pretty sketchy to me," I said.

"He'll be fine," she said.

We would be meth heads again. She was working on the costumes.

"He won't need one," I said.

"Ed has been off drugs for years," she said.

"Are you sure?" I said.

"I've known him for a long time."

She asked me to find a car and a gun for Ed.

"A gun?" I said. "Can he handle a gun?"

"I don't know. He's a Texan."

"Why does he even need a gun?"

She looked at me funny. "Why do we?"

"We've got enough guns," I said.

"But without a gun he won't look the part." She folded her arms like that settled that.

"I don't like it. How do you know he won't fuck up and shoot someone?"

"We could give him a gun with no bullets."

"You're going to send a man in there with a pistol and no ammunition?"

"Why not?"

"He might as well have his dick in his hand."

"Alex!" She laughed.

"You're setting him up to fail."

"Well?"

"Well what?"

"Well, we don't want to fail."

"I'll think about it."

It was about time to head to my gig. Ava decided to come with me.

"I've never seen you play," she said.

"You'll be bored," I said. "I'll be busy, and you won't have anyone to talk to."

"I want to hear you," she said.

"Cool," I said.

We went to my place to pick up my gear. I put on my torn up jeans with a different cowboy shirt, dark blue and satiny with embroidered roses.

"Wow, you look sharp," Ava said. "Got a hot date?"

"Yeah," I said and gave her a squeeze.

I put my gold top, Strat and amp in the car. I was already sweating. "Schlepping gear," I said. "The musician's curse."

"Yeah," she said, "I know schlepping."

We drove down to the club on Sixth Street like any other couple. We set up and did our sound check, then hung around back stage and drank a couple of beers and passed a joint. Ava looked at me funny when I took a hit, and I realized we'd never smoked together. I kind of shrugged and grinned. She passed.

The place started to fill up. When we went on, there was quite a crowd. Geoff was really doing a good job of getting his songs out there. These people were actually paying attention. After a while people started dancing. That rarely happens; we're not exactly a dance band. We were cooking. When people started dancing, we started stretching out. Randy and I were trading solos and feeding off each other. On the last song of the set he picked up my Strat and we found a groove, riffing off each other and rising to higher and higher reaches of the atmosphere. I bet we jammed on that song for 20 minutes. When we crashed the last chord the whole place erupted. People were on their feet, giving us a standing ovation. Us! That had to be a first. The applause went on and on. We were grinning at each other like idiots. Geoff had the presence of mind to put his hands over his heart and bow. The applause crescendoed.

People always come up between sets and want to talk and don't seem to realize the musicians actually need a break. A really cute girl was approaching Geoff when who should I see coming through the crowd but Beatriz.

Up popped up tall blonde with big tits on full display in a skimpy tube top. "I love the way you play," she said, "like you're making love to a woman."

She bent over and gave me a good look. "You're cute," she said. "Want to hang out after the show?"

"Yeah, maybe," I said. "I'm kind of with someone."

She shrugged like whatever and walked away.

I looked at Ava sitting in the back of the club. I tried to smile. She waved. Then Beatriz was there with hurt and reproach and longing written all over her.

"You are very good," she said. "I didn't even know you played."

"Thanks," I said.

Everyone else had left the stage. Geoff had his arm around the cutie and was heading for the bar; she couldn't have been over 21. I was standing there with my guitar around my neck looking like a fool but I kept it there because if I put it on the stand the next logical step would be I would have to give her a hug and it couldn't be just any kind of hug and that wouldn't do.

"How'd you, you know, know I'd be here?" I said.

"I had to read it in the newspaper," she said.

"It was in the newspaper?"

Her eyes were deep and dark. "Don't you want to see me?"

"Of course. I've been busy."

"Thinking?" she said.

"Yeah," I said, "thinking."

I didn't know what to say.

"Uh, maybe we can talk tomorrow," I said.

"Why not tonight, after your show?"

I glanced up. Ava was watching me intently.

"You are here with someone?" she said. She looked over her shoulder and scanned the crowd.

"Just a friend," I said. "Just the guys."

Her eyes were big and brimming. "I'm the one who loves you," she said.

"I know," I said.

"I'm carrying your baby."

"I know."

"I'm not just one of your whores," she said. She was wearing a tight, red, low-cut dress with a short, slit skirt. She turned to go.

"Tomorrow," I said.

She walked through the club with all the dignity she could muster. Every guy in the place had his eye on her. So did Ava.

In the second set, I was really off. I couldn't find the groove. My mind was all over the place. I let Randy have most of the solos. Geoff gave me a look.

After the show we packed up and drove home.

"Who was that?" she said.

"Who was what?" I said.

"That woman you were talking to."

"You'll have to be more specific," I said.

"During the break," she said.

"I don't know," I said. "That happens a lot."

"What?"

"Women come up to you after the show."

"Not the blonde," she said.

"Huh?" I said.

"The bombshell in the red dress," she said. "I wouldn't have said she's your type."

"What are you talking about?"

"That didn't look like any casual conversation."

"Some women can be pretty persistent," I said.

"I saw what you said."

"What?"

"Tomorrow."

"I did?"

"That's what you said."

"I may have. We have a gig tomorrow." I thought for a second. "No we don't."

"What were you talking about?"

"I don't know." I paused. "She wanted me to go home with her." That was true.

We pulled up in front of her house. I gave her a little cross-console hug and kiss.

"You know," she said, "today is the first day we've been together when we didn't make love."

"Is that a good thing or a bad thing?"

"I don't know," she said.

"You know, if we lived together, we could make love every day." I looked deep in her eyes. There were little lines around them. "Just so you know, I'm ready to marry you."

"Not so fast," she said. "I've got to have time to think. Let's finish this project and then we'll talk."

"I love you," I said.

"Love you too," she said. We kissed. She got out of the car.

"Good night," I said.

I went home and unloaded my gear in a kind of a trance. Inside, the little seal point was curled up in my chair. She studied me with those pale blue eyes that seemed to glow in the dark. "How did you get in here?" I said.

"Meep," she said. She hopped up and walked on her prim little feet to the door. I let her out.

I went straight to bed and lay there with iron discipline. Bugs were buzzing and birds were squawking outside my window all night long.

32

I got up at the crack of dawn and there she was again curled up in my chair.

"What are you doing?" I said.

"Meow," she said.

I started to pick her up to throw her out but she bolted for the studio. I followed. She was perched on the high window ledge, staring at me. I knew where this was headed. I went to the kitchen and made a cup of coffee and took it outside.

The air was almost cool this time of the morning. The lop-eared tabby brushed against my leg. The dove were cooing gently. As I was finishing my coffee, the little seal point showed up. I spent the next hour minutely inspecting the exterior of my house. It's not very big. I could discover no crack or crevice where a cat could come and go. I got my ladder and went up on the roof. I couldn't find anything. I gave up.

I called Beatriz about 8:30. She opened the door before I knocked. She sat me at the kitchen table and poured me a cup of coffee. She looked shy. She was wearing a thick dark robe that went down to her ankles, but she could never hide her beauty.

"Sorry I'm not dressed," she said. "I wasn't feeling so well."

"What's the matter?"

"Morning sickness," she said. She patted her tummy and smiled a thoughtful, self-satisfied little smile. "I'll be all right in a few minutes."

I took her to bed. There was nothing else to do. Under the robe she was wearing a sexy little nightie that came off at the first touch.

"You don't look any different," I said.

"Not yet," she said.

We were there for a couple of hours and, not to be too specific, there was this little thing she liked involving my fingers and my tongue and I had her writhing and screaming and sent her right over the moon.

I lay there exhausted for a while, then started to get up and put on my pants.

"Don't leave me," she said.

"I'm just going to the bathroom," I said.

She put her hand on my pants. "You won't need these," she said.

I went ahead and took care of business and came back and lay down beside her. She half-covered us with a sheet. It was too hot for a blanket.

"We need to talk," I said.

"We can talk here," she said. She was gently gripping me you know where.

"We can't talk here," I said.

"Just tell me how much you love me."

"I love you."

"I want you here with me forever and always."

She pulled on me ever so gently.

"And don't ever cheat on me again," she said. She kept pulling and squeezing. "I don't think I could stand it."

The next thing I was on top of her and kept at her till I sent her over the moon again.

I flopped over on my back breathing hard. She curled up next to me and took me in hand. "You don't know how much I love you," she said. "I don't ever want to let you go."

I gently disentangled myself, sat up and swung my legs off the side of the bed.

"This is not getting us anywhere," I said.

She wrapped her arms around me, put her head in my lap and started to work on me. Her passion was a powerful persuasion.

After another while went by we were lying there spent. She said, "I'll always love you. I'll never let you go. I'll never let you leave me."

"If we're going to be together..." I said. She was suddenly all ears and eyes. "I said if. There's some pretty important stuff I have to take care of first. Your client's not going to be too happy if we just—what? settle down? raise a family?"

"We can make it, baby," she said. "We can go out of state."

"We'll have to." I thought for a minute. "What's this meeting about.

"I don't know. He's expanding his operations, and he wants you to be part of the expansion. Apparently he likes your work."

"We'll have to wait till then."

"What will you do?"

"I don't know."

"That's what you have to think about?"

"Yeah."

"About us being together?"

"About how is it possible."

"Oh baby!" She hugged me with all her strength and buried her face in my chest.

I couldn't drag myself away until late in the afternoon. She was still clinging to me in the nude at the door. "Baby, you don't have to go. Stay here with me. I want you with me always."

"Not yet," I said.

I got to the car and drove away quick. It was only ten minutes home—less. I pulled onto my street and sitting there by the curb in her car was Ava.

I whipped into my driveway and took a deep breath before turning off the engine. I walked right over. She had the windows down and was kind of red-faced and sweating. I gave her a quick kiss. "Hey baby, how's it going?" I said.

She got out of her car. I gave her a hug. "Where have you been?" she said.

"Working, out," I said.

"You don't look like it," she said. I was wearing sandals, linen slacks and a silk t-shirt. "You don't smell like it."

"Let's go inside," I said. "Let's don't stand out here in the heat."

She shook her head. "Oh god."

"This was work related," I said.

She looked skeptical.

"She came on to me," I said.

She still didn't believe me.

"Come on," I said.

We went inside.

"How long has this been going on," she said. "Oh god, I hope you've been using protection."

"Nothing happened," I said.

"You said…"

"She came on to me but nothing happened. I didn't let anything happen."

"I smelled her perfume."

"Like I said, she came on to me."

I took her in my arms. "You need a shower," she said.

"You're the one I want," I said. "You know I love you. You know how I feel about you."

She walked across the room and turned around. She crossed her arms.

"I thought you said you're not working," she said.

"I'm not."

"But she's part of that?"

"These people are persistent."

"Persistent. You said that."

"Yeah."

"She works for them?"

"Yeah."

"She looks like a whore," she said. "I mean, I'm not into slut shaming, but I mean." She laughed. She gave me a hug and a kiss. "You stink," she said. "Go, take a shower."

I did. I stalled around checking my email and whatever for a bit first, then I took a long, long hot shower. I took a long time primping and powdering and getting dressed.

"Hey, I'm starving," I said. "Let's get something to eat."

We went to an elegant Chinese place way across town. I ordered in series, dragging out the meal. We had a nice pinot gris. I lingered over my wine. I needed time, and I didn't want to get drunk. I spent about 500 dollars with tip. We went home.

I took her to bed and showed her how much I loved her. Nothing epic, but I managed to satisfy her. I don't want to go into detail, but I did this little thing with tongue and fingers she liked and all was good. I rolled over in bed after that and must have fallen asleep.

I woke up later. She was sprawled on her side with barely a corner of the sheet covering her midsection. I slipped out of bed and turned on the lamp on the dresser. It's not very bright. I crept back into bed and studied her. God, how I loved her. I wanted to swallow her, to absorb her, all of her confidence and certainty and talent. I wanted to spend the rest of my life with her, remember. I studied the lines of her face. I studied the little stretch marks beside her boobs and suddenly wondered if she had any kids. I studied the color of her hair. The colors. Red and gold and tawny and sandy and onyx and amber and shining silver. I wondered how old she was.

I studied her for a long time. I slipped out of bed. I turned off the light. I went to the bathroom. I crawled into bed. I curled up next to her. I started kissing the back of her neck and fondling her breasts. I hugged her and kissed her and touched her and brought her awake. We made sweet and passionate love and thus I proved to her how much I loved her.

"You don't know how much I love you," I said.

"Mmm," she said. She patted me on the hand, rolled over and went back to sleep.

33

I didn't sleep much, or well. At first light I was up. I made myself a cup of coffee and went into the living room. The seal point was in my chair and the lop-eared tabby was on the couch.

"What do you want?" I said.

The tabby chirped like a bird. The seal point just stared at me with those bright blue eyes. I sat down on the couch. Nobody moved. I drank my coffee.

I could hear Ava in the bathroom. She came into the living room and looked us over. "How'd you sleep?" she said.

"Well," I said.

She looked us over again, taking our measure. "Let's sit outside," she said.

I made some more coffee and we went out to the garden. It was still early enough to be cool, or at least not hot.

"You know," she said, "I know that I don't really have any say about who you fool around with. You've come on so strong, and I haven't been ready to make any kind of commitment. We haven't really known each other very long."

"I feel like I've known you forever."

"Look, I get it. You're a good-looking guy, movie-star good-looking. Women throw themselves at you. You'd have to be a saint. You're under no obligation. But, you know, from the way you talk…"

"I meant every word of it. I'd marry you today."

"I know. That scares me. Been there, done that."

"You never told me you were married."

"You never asked. I don't like to talk about it. I don't like to think about it."

"Oh?"

"We married young." Something about the way she said that made her sound old. She looked into the empty street. "We made a commitment. We were actually serious about our commitment. We believed in it. There was no infidelity or violence or anything. We were both too nice for that. We truly loved each other. But it wasn't enough. We tried and we tried and we tried until we were exhausted, but we just couldn't make ourselves into someone who could please, satisfy, fulfill the expectations of, whatever, of the other. Especially as we grew and matured, we only became more and more like ourselves and those selves just weren't right for each other. Does any of that even make any sense?"

"I think so."

"The divorce was really painful, but, you know, in retrospect, it was the right thing to do, it was the only thing to do, even though, you know, I would still, I guess I should say I still love him."

"Where is he?"

"He passed away five years later. ALS. He wasn't even 40. I was already building my new life, but I helped him all I could during, well, his whole decline. It was horrible. He had to watch himself die a little bit at a time. It was inspiring, really, his courage. That's when I realized that I still loved him, would always love him. He was a good man, a kind person, a gentle soul."

"Any kids?"

She smiled and wiped away a tear. "My beautiful Gracie. She would be 20."

"What happened?" I said.

"A car wreck. She was with her dad."

"Oh my god."

"That's when we found out about the ALS, when he was in the hospital. It wasn't his fault. A drunk driver."

"I'm so sorry."

"Oh, I'm at peace with the divorce and his death, believe me. But her death, that's a pain I carry with me always."

"How old are you?"

She looked at me quickly. "I'm 43."

She watched me for a reaction.

"How about you?" she said.

I hesitated for the tiniest fraction of a second. I added a couple of years just to make her feel better. I've always wanted to be honest in this relationship, but I didn't want her thinking that I was thinking she was too old for me. "I'm 38," I said.

"I mean, were you ever married?"

"No. I've moved around a lot. I've done a couple of stints overseas, kind of off the radar, you know. I've had a couple or few live-ins, but just when, you know, we'd start to get something established I'd have to up stakes and move on. Sometimes on pretty short notice."

"Any kids?"

"Not that I know of." I kind of laughed.

She sipped her coffee and made a face. "It's cold," she said, and tossed it in the grass. She stood up; so did I. "I'm so glad we had this conversation," she said.

"Me too," I said. I hugged her.

We pulled apart. "I just think, I want to thank you, for giving me more time. I think that, after this weekend, you know, after next week, I'll have a lot more time. And woe to any director who says this, but I think the hardest part of the production will be behind me. I mean there will still be a lot of work but I'll move on to interiors and stuff like that where I have more control and my life will be, I think, a lot more normal." She laughed. "When has my life ever been normal?"

I didn't know what to say to that so I kissed her.

"Well, I've got a lot to get done this week. I better go."

I kissed her again. "Me too."

She looked kind of funny.

"I have a lot to get done, too."

34

I jogged, swam or rode my bike for a couple of hours every day that week and I started feeling a lot better. I found a 20-something-year-old van with no title that was pretty beat-up but ran good. I bought it from an old boy for $600 and he looked glad to get it. It was Thursday, so I stashed it in a pay-to-park garage.

I went to a gun show in Cedar Park, a suburb of Austin that really reminds you what mainstream America is all about. Everybody at this place was at least 40 pounds overweight—men, women and children. If you've never been to a gun show, you probably think the people who go to gun shows are a bunch of gun nuts, but the truth is a lot of these guys are lawyers and dentists, guys with disposable income. And shooting is a family sport. Kids love it, especially boys. It's more fun that fireworks.

A lot of people think bigger is better, but I didn't want to give old Ed anything too quick or too powerful, just like I wouldn't put him in a Ferrari unless I was sure he knew how to drive it. I found him a single-action revolver, like an old cowboy pistol, Italian made, a replica, chambered for .38 special. It was perfect. It looked intimidating, but Ed wouldn't be able to shoot the place up accidentally with it, it was just too slow and cumbersome. It was in good shape—there's hardly anything to go wrong with a revolver. And it was single-action, which means you have to cock it by pulling back the hammer each time you fire it.

I was a little nervous, so I drove up to Jewell just to see that everything was as it was. I pulled off the interstate and cruised slowly past the first—eastern —bank. It was the Friday before Labor Day, so they were busy. Next time anyone could transact any business there would be Tuesday. I idled through the U-turn chute and cruised past the second bank. They were busy too. Busy here meant three or four cars in the parking lot. I pulled into the convenience store. I figured what the hell, it had been months since I had been here in the Beamer. If I stopped here twice, so might anyone who made frequent or not-so-frequent trips between Austin or San Antonio and Dallas.

I picked up a bottle of water and took it to the front. At the counter, among the impulse-buys, was a line of locally made jerky. I picked up a bag of spicy venison. There was a pimply, overweight teenager at the register. "So how is life here in Jewell?" I said.

"Nothing ever happens here," he said.

I started to ask him if he worked on Tuesdays, but checked myself. Still, I couldn't help but smile.

I cruised around the back roads looking for likely places. The countryside is more heavily populated than you think. You can actually do better trying to hide something in an urban location than out in the country, where anything new or out of place will be noticed.

I drove home in a contemplative mood, sucking on that jerky. It was strong and hot. I didn't want to admit it, but something was bothering me. I didn't want to be petty or anything, but, I mean, Ava was 7 years older than me—at least. I wondered if she had lied about her age, as women will. I knew she wouldn't have added to the total. Not that that made any difference, or course. I wanted to marry her.

That was Friday. Saturday, I rented a silver Chevy four-door, called Ava and went over to see Beatriz. I figured I about had to.

Sunday and Monday I worked out. I guess you could say Beatriz was a workout, too. Monday afternoon I went over to Ava's. She had everything together on her end. She had Ed all lined out, she said. We packed up and stopped off at the local upscale pizza place for a nice relaxing dinner. We had a nice pizza with crab and scallops, feta, sun-dried tomatoes and red onions in a ricotta sauce with a couple of lager beers.

Back at the house we looked over the props and costumes. She had made a funny cap for me with long, greasy, tangled gray hair sewn in that hung down to my shoulders. "I'll give you some wrinkles and stubble in the morning. You'll look 20 years older." She looked me over. "Thirty."

I showed her the gun. It was big and bulky. "Wow," she said. "That looks dangerous."

"It is," I said.

We went to bed early and got up early. I barely slept. The bugs and the birds were going all night long. The seal point and the lop-ear were sleeping on my chair and the sofa, respectively.

I put on overalls over a pair of yuppie shorts, and a silk t-shirt under a nasty old work shirt. With my long hair, whiskers and meth sores, I really did look the part. She put on a pair of coveralls she had sewn a bunch of padding in that completely concealed her curves. She stuck her hair up under a hat like mine, only the long greasy hair hanging down was dark. She gave herself a mustache and that eradicated her gender, if you didn't look too closely at her hands.

We left before light. We wanted to get there about 9, when we still had a crowd. Don't ask me—Ava needed a crowd in her scene.

We picked up the van at the parking garage. I paid at one of those electronic kiosks and had to use my credit card, but I figured what the hell, anybody might have occasion to park here. We picked up Ed at his bus stop before the buses were running. He was wearing stained camo pants.

I gave Ed his gun. "Be careful," I said.

"I know how to handle a gun," he said.

Ava and I took the rental; Ed followed in the van. We pulled off the highway at this little place I had found. A dirt road ran alongside the highway to a creek and veered off to the right, ending at a little turnaround above a canyon choked with brush. We stashed the rental and jumped in the van. I was driving. Ava, on the passenger's side, activated the cameras. Ed crouched down in back and held onto Ava's seat.

I took our exit and rolled up on the first bank. There were five or six cars in the parking lot. I found a spot close to the front and we swept in guns drawn. I took the manager back to the vault. Ava and Ed kept the crowd covered. There was one security guard who looked to be about 85. He never moved from his chair. I came out behind the manager, who had a bag in each hand. Ed and Ava each grabbed a bag and we were out the door and in the van within 10 seconds. I took off north on the frontage road going slow so they could see me, crowned the little rise and whipped around the U-turn under the freeway out of sight. I turned into the parking lot of the second bank where there were six or seven cars. We pulled into a spot just as a security guard was coming out of the front door. He was a cowboy about 60 who was definitely not in the mainstream. He walked past us saying, "Would you look at that."

Across the freeway a police car lights flashing drove at high speed the wrong way on the frontage road and whipped into the bank parking lot. A couple of seconds later a highway patrol car went flying north siren wailing. We ducked inside the bank and flashed our guns. I took the manager to the vault and came out quick with a couple of bags. The customers were thoroughly cowed. The security guard was still outside. We broke for the van. The manager stuck his head out the door and yelled, "Hey!"

We had made the van when the guard came around the back. Ava got behind the wheel and I took cover behind the passenger's door. Ed threw down on the guard and told him to put up his hands. He looked Ed over coolly, saw his gun wasn't cocked, and slowly started to draw his own black automatic. Ed was fumbling with the hammer. The guard was calmly undoing the hammer strap on his holster. Ed got his gun cocked and got off a round, then another, which impacted the pavement and the car next to us. This all happened in less than half a second. The guard fired and broke out the window where I was standing, then fired again and Ed slumped against the van. By this time I had my piece in play and I put two rounds into the guard. The first went through his forearm and he dropped his gun. The second hit him in the thigh and knocked him down. I slid open the door, threw Ed inside, jumped in behind and yelled, "Go!"

Ava floored it and jumped over a curb before regaining the frontage road and careening onto the freeway. We flew south for a couple of minutes and took our exit. "Careful," I said.

She slowed down. We crossed the overpass, turned north and took our little dirt road. There was the Chevy, just waiting for us. We had been all of seven minutes.

We jumped out of the van. I rolled Ed over. He was bleeding all over the place and struggling for breath.

Ava was crying. "What'll we do?" she said.

"Change," I said. We shucked our costumes and threw them in the van. Ed wasn't breathing any more. I took his min-cam and gun without getting blood on me. The money bags were sopping. Ava reached for them. "Leave it," I said. I closed the door. We rolled the van over the edge of the canyon; it crashed down into the brush. It was pretty well hidden, I thought.

Ava just stood there staring, looking lost. "Get in the car," I said. We got back on the freeway going north. "They'll be looking south now," I said.

We drove to Waco and had lunch according to plan. We were sitting in a nice restaurant overlooking the river. "I don't feel like eating," Ava said.

"Just order a salad," I said.

I got the chicken-fried steak, the most generic thing on the menu. It was awful, but I forced myself to eat it. We dawdled over lunch for an hour. I figured that was about right.

We got back on the freeway heading south. North of Jewell we passed a checkpoint on the northbound side, and south of town we got stuck in a long line of traffic. When we came to the checkpoint, the cop waved us through.

She wiped her eyes. "I can't believe he's dead," she said.

"This ain't over," I said.

"What do you mean?" she said.

"When they find him, they'll tie him to you."

"I don't think so."

"Somebody will miss him."

"I don't think so."

"Doesn't he have a girlfriend or something?"

"Not really. Kind of."

"Won't she miss him?"

"She'll just think he's disappeared again."

"Huh?"

"Ed had a way of kind of falling off the wagon and going off."

"Yeah? For how long?"

"Weeks. Months. I don't know. Last time he was homeless for over a year."

"Great! You brought a homeless guy?"

"You should be glad."

"I'm ecstatic."

"Poor Ed. At least I'll miss him."

"You're pretty cool about the whole thing."

"Look, I loved Ed like a brother. Or a crazy cousin. He was special." She shook her head. "That's why we called him Special Ed." She laughed sadly.

"You brought along a crazy guy."

"He knew what he was getting into."

"What did you tell him?"

"He was doing what he loved."

"Robbery?"

"No. Acting."

We got home early. We took the rental to the agency and picked up sandwiches on the way back. We ate while we reviewed the footage. We had three separate views of the whole thing. Ed's camera had picked up an incredible shot of the shot that killed him and of the guard going down under my bullets.

"This is horrible," Ava said.

"No shit," I said.

Inside the van Ed's camera was pointed at the ceiling. The audio captured his last ragged breath.

"Oh my god," she said.

"We have to destroy it," I said.

"No! It's perfect," she said.

"You're kidding."

"This is exactly what I've been going for."

"What, a murder?"

"We didn't murder anyone."

"When anyone dies during the commission of a felony, it's murder. It's called the felony murder rule."

"Well, I have to use that part."

"This is no longer a movie," I said. "This is serious."

"I'm very serious about my movie," she said.

"Deadly serious?"

"Obviously."

"What about the part when I tell you to leave the money. No one would believe that."

"I'll just cut around it."

"At the end there, you can see the rental."

"That I'll destroy."

I yawned. She did too. Her faced looked haggard and old.

"God, I'm exhausted," she said.

"Want to stay with me?" I said.

"No," she said. "I think I'd rather be alone."

35

I went to bed. I knew I couldn't sleep, but I needed the rest. Through the sheer force of will I lay flat on my back. The bugs and birds were going at it non-stop. I could hear the cats running around in the living room. I may have slept a bit during the crepuscular hour.

I had a cup of coffee with the cats, then walked the couple of blocks to the new kolache shop. I got apricot, which is supposed to be a classic, but I couldn't eat half of it—it was just too sweet.

I took a long hot shower and finished with cold to clear the cobwebs. Then I remembered the ultimate cobweb clearer, and thought what the hell. I got out a jar and cut out a couple of big lines. Those were so good I did a couple more. I filled my bullet, then I called Beatriz and went over there and did the usual. I did it to keep her on board, of course, but mainly I did it for me. I didn't want to think. Beatriz was the best antidote to rational thought I ever found.

Beatriz, all by herself, was enough for any man. She was so pure of heart. With all that talent and that special skill, she lifted me above my own level and put me to work even when I was played out. With the help of my traveler, we set new records.

Nevertheless, there were lulls, of course. At one point, I was lying there on my back keeping perfectly still while she rested her head on my shoulder and snored softly. It was an endearing snore, so innocent and unselfconscious. I found myself thinking of Ava. I kept wondering what she must think about the age difference. I mean, seven years is a long time, like almost half a generation. Seven years at minimum. I wondered how many years she shaved off her age. Supposedly she's five years older than me. But she's already cutting two or three years or who knows how much, so we're back to seven or who knows even ten and then there's the two years I added to my age she doesn't even know about. Was she thinking I was too young for her? I mean, we grew up listening to different songs on the radio, stuff like that. When I hit 40 she'll be 50 and she must be worried that she'll no longer be attractive to me, or maybe that I don't have the maturity to fully appreciate a woman of her maturity.

It felt so natural and right I stayed there in bed with Beatriz for the next three days. When we ate, we ate in bed. I didn't need clean underwear because I hadn't worn my underwear fifteen minutes before they landed on the bedroom floor. I used her toothbrush. We really got a lot closer.

At one point I thought I might as well find out what more I could about next week's meeting with Johnson.

"I am not privy to the details of his enterprises, except in a general way of course. I don't know anything except what I've told you. He wants to talk to you about something not exactly in your line of work—your former line of work—but something related. Something bigger. He said he likes your work."

I was just going to this meeting out of curiosity and to keep from offending Johnson, but I have to admit, I was flattered. That was stupid, I know. But in my former line of work no one ever sees your work in its entirety, except you yourself.

I slept really well when I slept there beside her, and when I lay awake I took comfort from her warmth.

At one point, I thought to ask her about herself. Her story was more or less as I'd guessed. "My mother was a prostitute in Nuevo Laredo. My father was puro castellano, she said. That's where I got this white skin, she always said. Mama was muy morena, you know, pura india. That's where I got this fat ass."

I said, "Your ass is a lot of things, baby, but fat's not one of them." She smiled.

Her mother sent her to live with an aunt and go to school in Laredo, but that was the time when the reach of the cartels was growing. She was forced into prostitution when she was 14. That's how she came to the notice of El Cuarenta. She belonged exclusively to him for three years, until he tired of her. But he had seen something in her. Rather than send her back to the brothels, he sent her to college in Houston and to law school in Austin.

"When he fell, he had been my sole client ever since I passed the bar, three years ago. Of course, with my resume, my previous clientele, I could only look for certain kinds of clients. I was retained by my present client in July."

"So you don't know him any better than I do."

"I suppose that's true.

We went back to work. When it came time to go, I didn't want to go. I stood up and put on my underwear. "Stay with me," she whispered.

"I've got business to take care of," I said. I finished dressing.

She put on her robe, followed me to the door and clung to me. "Take care, my love," she said.

36

I went home. I checked on-line. The Dallas, Houston and Austin papers had all picked it up—just a short squib that made it seem almost like a joke. The security guard survived. They hadn't found Ed or the van. That was good. The longer he lay there the better. Let the weather, bugs and birds degrade and destroy the evidence.

I didn't have any business to take care of that I knew of. I figured I needed to check in with Ava, keep her on board. These women! They'll do any lying, manipulative thing to get their way. My phone was dead, I'm sure, but I had no idea where it was and I didn't feel like looking for it. She wouldn't want to be bothered at this hour. "Fuck it!" I said. "I'll go over there any time I please."

I took a shower to remove any traces of Beatriz. I did a couple of fat lines and reloaded my bullet. I wanted to have plenty of energy, to get past the thought that she was in her late 40s, or beyond. I drove to her place in five minutes and parked in front. I took a couple of quick toots and looked in the rearview mirror to make sure there was no residue on my nose hairs. I strode up the walk and knocked on the door.

She took a while to answer. I was standing out there in the heat kind of bouncing on my toes. When she opened the door, I could hardly recognize her. She was wearing a frumpy old Mother Hubbard housedress and her hair was kind of half caught up in a bun.

"Hey, baby," I said, real smooth.

"Hey," she said, "where've you been? I've been trying to call."

"I lost my phone, I think."

I stepped inside and gave her a hug so I wouldn't have to look at her.

"How've you been?" I said.

"Kind of weepy," she said. "Kind of scared."

I had to look at her then. She looked worried. That made the lines in her face all the more noticeable.

"There's been hardly anything in the news," I said.

"I haven't seen anything," she said.

"They don't have anything," I said.

I figured I better get it over with. I took her to bed. I got her out of that ugly assed old woman's dress. At least her body was still looking good. I went to work getting her ready. I was still in my pants. I got up and started to the bathroom. "Be right back," I said.

I took a couple of quick hits from the traveler, washed my face, shucked my jeans and tried to pee but couldn't. I flushed anyway and went back to bed. I don't like to kiss and tell but I closed my eyes and gave her my best shot. She seemed to enjoy it.

She rolled over on her side, facing away from me. I could see how much gray she had in her hair. I rubbed her neck, to reassure her, you know, let her know I still cared.

She rolled over my way. I rolled on my back and looked at the ceiling. "You know honey," she said. "I've been thinking more about what we said."

"Hmm?"

"I think I'm ready," she said.

"For what?" I said.

"To make at commitment," she said.

I looked at her. "You want to get married?" I said.

"I don't know about that," she said. "Why don't we just move in together?"

"I don't know about that," I said. "I think we better hold off a little while. We've got this thing hanging over our heads. I think we ought to let it cool off a little while before we make any sudden change."

"I thought you said they don't have anything."

"We don't want to give anybody any reason to think anything."

"This was your idea."

"Where were you thinking of?"

"Well, my lease is coming up, so I figured I could just move in with you."

"I don't think so. If you move into my house, you'll always feel like you're in my house, just like I would if I moved into your house, you know? No. We need to find a place that will be our house."

"How long will that take?"

"I don't know. I'll want to do a few touch ups on my place before I put it on the market."

"That'll take months. Just think of all the money we can save if we move in together."

"I don't care about that," I said. "Do you need money?"

"I will. Pretty soon."

"It's five minutes away."

"I'll come over later," she said. "Maybe tomorrow."

"Want to get something to eat?"

"Nah, I'm not hungry."

"What are you doing right now?"

"I guess I'll crawl back into the editing cave."

"Huh?"

"You know, as sorry as I am about Ed, I'm more excited about the movie."

"What do you mean?"

"The footage is fantastic."

"But you can't use it."

"Of course I can."

"It's incriminating evidence."

"I can work around that."

"So you're exploiting your friend's death? That's kind of cold."

"What are you talking about? It's the role of a lifetime."

"Role? He never said a line."

"Just exactly like I told him. This is his best work on film."

"He didn't do anything—except fuck up and nearly get us killed."

"We rehearsed for three days. He was in character, and he stayed in character, right to the end. That's acting."

"This is crazy," I said.

37

I went home. I ran a hot bath and cut out a couple of fat lines. I lay back in the hot water. Every nerve ending was alive. My mind was supercharged to a sort of super-consciousness. From a vast height I saw to the farthest horizon with infinite clarity. All things were laid out before me.

Ava would never approve of even the most judicious use of cocaine, I felt certain from the way she looked at me when we passed that joint backstage before the show. The heavy lines in her face when she frowned reminded me of my mother. She was really starting to show her age.

The seal point stepped into the bathroom on her dainty little feet. I regarded her from my lofty perspective. She jumped on the toilet—the lid was down—and now she was at eye-level. She stared at me with those penetrating eyes.

"What do you want?" I said.

She stuck out her tiny pink tongue. "Meep," she said.

The bath was going tepid. I let out some of the water and refreshed it nice and hot from the tap. I took a couple of toots from my bullet to maintain my elevated vantage point. The cat posed like a sphinx and watched my every action. I lay back and closed my eyes. I thought of Ava and I thought of Beatriz. I thought of Beatriz and I thought of Ava. From time to time I peeked at the cat. She was watching me closely. I refreshed the bath water again. I lay there a long time. I peeked at her. She was staring.

"Stop reading my mind," I said.

She jumped up and ran out of the bathroom. I got out of the tub and dried off. I could hear something in the living room. I stepped into a pair of gym shorts and went to look. The cats froze. There were four of them—the seal point kitten, the lop-eared tabby, an orange tabby and the tuxedo from across the street, I think. They stared. I just stood there. The seal point was crouched on the floor, the orange perched on the back of the couch, the tuxedo sat at attention on my chair, and the lop-ear was on top of the bookshelf. I backed off. They watched me go. I slipped into the kitchen and waited a few seconds before sneaking to the other door and peeking at them. They were playing a funny game. The seal point stalked imperceptibly. The other cats watched her. Suddenly she sprang. The other three jumped and all changed places, like musical chairs. Now the seal point was standing arch-backed on the couch, the lop-ear was in my chair, feigning indifference, the tuxedo was on the coffee table and the orange cat was crouching on the floor and starting her stalk. They did this three or four times. I wanted to play. I crept out of the kitchen and stalked the tuxedo who was now stalking. I sprang. They bolted for the studio. I followed them, laughing and making little cat-noises. I heard a crash and bong. They had taken high positions on the window sills. I was in the habit of leaving guitars out on stands; I had no kids or pets, and I wanted my studio to be ready to plug in and play. Now I was standing there staring at my 1959 gold top Les Paul face down on the floor with a broken headstock. We're talking a 30,000-dollar instrument. I dropped to my knees and gently turned it over like a drowning child and I was about to perform artificial respiration—too late. The guitar lay there cold and unresponsive. Tears filled my eyes. In sudden fear I glanced at my '64 Strat—literally, the best Stratocaster I've ever played, and another 20 K. The top was scoured and scraped through the aged sonic blue finish and deep into the wood, and the beautiful dark rosewood fretboard was ravaged. The goddamn bastards had been using it as a scratching post. My tears turned to rage. I stormed into the living room. They were nowhere to be seen. I went to my room and got my gun. I searched the entire house and couldn't find the goddamn cats. I went back into the living room and there they were. I opened fire. The cats leapt and flew. I kept shooting. I really wanted to mangle and kill the little bastards, but I could barely see for the tears in my eyes. Then I was out of bullets, and I had eight neat little holes in the ceiling, wall and beautiful hardwood floor. The cats were somewhere, I don't know where.

I sat on the floor crying for a long time, then there was a knock at the door. I thought it must be the cops. I peeked out the peephole—it was Ava. "Just a minute," I said and ran to my room. I put up the pistol and went to the bathroom to wash my face. I was still wiping my eyes with a towel when I opened the door.

"What's wrong?" she said.

"Nothing," I said.

She looked at me closely. "What's the matter? Are you all right?"

"The goddamn cats," I said. "They ruined my guitars." I almost started crying again.

"Cats?" she said. "You have cats?"

"You were here the other day, you saw them."

"I did?"

"They were right here!"

"Take it easy," she said, putting her hand on my shoulder. "Honestly? I honestly don't remember."

I was exerting every ounce of strength I had to retain my self-control. "They're not really my cats," I said. "They're more like neighborhood cats."

"And you let them come inside?"

"They found a way. I need to call someone."

She looked at the ceiling. She looked at the wall. She looked at the floor. "What happened here?" she said.

"I wanted to kill them," I said.

"You shot them?"

"At them."

"You shot at them."

"They fucked up my guitars!"

"Can't they be replaced?"

"No."

"Can they be repaired?"

"They'll never be the same."

"Come with me," she said. She took me to the bedroom. "Lie down and let mama take care."

I lay face down. She straddled me and started massaging my back, neck and shoulders. It felt good. I groaned. A couple of tears leaked onto the pillow. She rolled me on my back and slipped her hand into my shorts. "Just let mama take care of everything," she said.

She worked on me for quite a while but there was nothing doing and that was that. No amount of cocaine in the world could lift me now. "Oh baby," she said, "it's all right. Don't worry about it."

"I'm still upset," I said.

"You need to relax. They were just guitars. It's not like you lost a loved one or something."

"Yes it is," I said. "It's exactly like that."

"I don't think I've ever seen you this emotional."

"No two guitars are alike. They're living, breathing—they have souls."

I rolled over and she rubbed my back some more.

"Oh, I forgot," she said.

"About what?" I said.

"About the money. That's why I came over in the first place."

"What money?"

"You remember. I said I'd come over."

I jumped out of bed and grabbed a handful of hundreds. "How's that?" I said.

"Fine," she said.

She left, thank god. I lay there on my back staring at the ceiling. I was thinking how much she looked like my mother when she disapproved of something. Suddenly I remembered when I was a boy there was a cat—a big orange cat. I don't know whether it was ours or a neighbor's or whose or nobody's. It was ragged and mangy and mean, but it would come right up to me and rub against me and purr and let me pet it all over and pull its tail. It used to follow me around, and one day I ran in the house and let the screen door slam behind me like Mama was always telling me not to and caught that cat right on the neck and killed it then and there. Something made me turn around and look. It was lying there head stuck in the door so still and awkward and silent. I couldn't understand what happened. Mama came then, pushed open the door and touched the cat. She frowned a deep and mysterious frown.

"Oh Billie," she said, "what have you done?"

38

I wrapped myself in my sheet and kept perfectly still. The bugs and birds were my friends. I heard the cats in the living room. I got up and shut my door. I just didn't want to fuck with anybody's shit right now. I was taut as a spring, and watchful. Something was approaching, something big surging just below the horizon.

I rose at dawn to a different light. I felt great. I was powerful and visionary, merciful and compassionate. Perfect just the way I was. I didn't need cocaine. I needed exercise.

The morning was cool with maybe that first hint of autumn. Not that the temperature changed, but maybe the humidity, just a little. I went for a jog. I've always remembered an old psych prof I had who maybe was so close to retirement he didn't give a shit, I don't know, but he would really strip away the pseudo-scientific bullshit theories and get right down to simple common sense; funny old guy always cracking jokes about Freud and Jung, the college administration, politics, whatever, if everybody could have attended his classes it would have put 99 percent of psychologists out of business. What he said about stress I've always remembered. If you're experiencing stress, there are three things you can do to handle it: 1) you can change your circumstances, 2) you can change your attitude, or 3) you can exercise. But you can't always change your circumstances—say your parents are dying, or two different women are mad to marry you. If you don't think that's stressful, try it. As for changing your attitude, that doesn't work any better. If you hate your job or your spouse, it's pretty unlikely that you're going to wake up the next day loving it or him or her. But exercise—that works every time. And that's the only thing that's bothering me—I've been under a little stress.

I went jogging around the neighborhood. I was out there in the light and air with the squirrels and birds and butterflies. Everything was parched. I couldn't help feeling encouraged by the flowers that struggled so hard to bloom in the heat.

I got home. I glanced at the studio but couldn't bear the thought of going in there or even looking. I put on my helmet and got on my bike and went to the tacqueria where I ate a potato and egg taco. Then I went for a nice long cruise, a couple of hours at an easy pace, just dogging it. When I got home it was getting hot so I jumped in the car and drove down to Deep Eddy. I swam a few laps, lay out in the sun, then swam a few more. I sat on the side of the pool and air-dried. The sky was full of light, every molecule aglow. On the drive home, I felt great. I was full of energy yet calm and in control. Even the traffic didn't bother me.

I showered, and toweling off caught myself in the mirror looking good. Any woman would be privileged to get a piece of this, I thought. I thought of calling Beatriz. Then I remembered the business I needed to take care of. I was only going out of curiosity and maybe a bit of an ego rush, but I figured I ought to check out the meeting place beforehand anyhow.

I dressed kind of nice casual and drove out to the restaurant by the lake. It was an upscale Tex-Mex restaurant, but let's face it, when the basis of everything is beans and rice it's hard to talk about upscale. The place was all deck, or rather decks, a series descending a good 200 feet down the slope to a steep drop-off. I went down to check it out. The lake, what was left of it, looked like a river running through a desert canyon. On this side was a deep pool at the bottom of a cliff, maybe 20 feet to the water. I took a table out in the open, about in the middle; some of the decks were pretty well screened with juniper and scrub oaks and I assumed that's where we'd meet. Everything was expensive, but what did I care? I started with a margarita with 100 percent blue agave tequila (note: all tequila is 100 percent blue agave) that cost 15 bucks. I didn't need it, but I enjoyed it. Then I had the shrimp fajitas, which were overcooked and over 30 dollars, not that I gave a shit. The view was good and the sunset fantastic. Vultures turned lazy circles in a sky that went from deep purple to pale blue to bright gold to orange to deep flaming crimson. The hills were tranquil and soothing if barren and dry. The vastness and infinite patience of nature filled me with benign affection and indulgence for everything and everyone. We're all suffering creatures just trying to make it through one day at a time. My stresses were the result of my choices. I had chosen, or let others choose for me, which amounted to the same thing. Everything happens for a reason, even if we don't always know the reason or the reason turns out to be somebody's cheap bullshit or your own or maybe God hates you and you should never have been born. As the earth spun like a wobbling top and the sun sank ever-so-slowly behind the hills I began to think that the mystics were right, that time and space are but an illusion, even though here and now in this mortal frame we are bound and chained to both dimensions.

As for the guitars, I had to admit they could be replaced. They wouldn't be the same, but I could lose and grieve and love again. It wouldn't be cheap, but what did I care about money? I had money burning a hole in my pocket.

The broken headstock and ruined finish could be repaired; they wouldn't be original but still I could sell the instruments to someone who didn't have that history with them, if I wanted, at a loss of course but who really cares? As for the cats, I had to admit I still liked them a little. I would be sorry if I hurt them, living creatures, on account of something artificial, however precious.

I drove home reflecting on the emptiness of existence. I was supposed to be retired. Why did I have to work so hard to please everyone? I was starting to like not having a cell phone.

I got home and went manfully into the studio. The gold top was lying there forlorn. I kneeled and cradled it in my arms. It had given me a lot of years of faithful service. I looked at the break. It didn't look as bad as I thought. In fact, it didn't appear to be broken at all. Only the nut was cracked—an easy fix. I couldn't believe it. I looked at the Strat, still on its stand. The scratches didn't seem that bad. I looked more closely. I couldn't see them at all. I got a flashlight and got down on my knees. Those massive scratches were the same old nicks and dings in the finish that was, after all, in excellent condition for a 50-year-old instrument, and the fretboard looked like it just needed a good oiling. It must have been a trick of the light. I felt like an idiot.

I put the guitars in their cases and went into the living room. The bullet holes were there all right and very real.

39

I went to bed and lay as still as I could as long as I could. That gave me time to think. The bugs and the birds did their thing. They're my friends, they're more than friends, but they can be annoying.

I thought and I thought and I thought and I thought. I've always been one to plan ahead, gather intelligence, map out strategy and tactics, prepare the field and control the moment of action. I worked very hard and very smart and very successfully for a very long time in a demanding, risky and stressful profession. Here I was supposedly enjoying my well-deserved retirement and I was worn out with thinking and hoping and wishing and worrying. Why did I have to decide everything for everybody? If everything happens for a reason, if we are the result of our choices, the reasons are often obscure and the choices seemingly insignificant. If I can't control everything, maybe that's just the universe's way of telling me I'm not in control. I'm not the one in charge. I don't have to take responsibility for anyone's behavior except my own, and even that's iffy. Better lay back, take things easy, go with the flow. I would hear Johnson out, give him the polite brush-off, go back to my life of retirement and let things take care of themselves.

Much as it pained me, I thought I could see which way the whole Ava v. Beatriz thing was likely to go. I was tired of Austin anyway. Maybe I would go back to Florida. I could probably find a sleepy little beach town where we could hang out, drink beer and eat good seafood. That might be cool. Or Mexico. Or maybe Brazil. Nobody would know me there.

I got up at first light. I went to the kitchen and there on the counter was my cell phone big as life. I had to laugh. I stood there staring at it a minute or two. Wouldn't it be better to let it lie? I plugged in the charger and the thing struggled to life. A whole bunch of missed calls and texts pinged onto the screen. I would look at them later.

I made a cup of coffee and went into the living room. The little seal point was neatly curled on the couch, staring at me with those bright blue eyes.

"Sorry," I said.

"Maui," she said.

I sat on the couch next to her. She let me pet her. She purred almost inaudibly. That's real love. No grasping or clinging, wanting nothing, needing nothing, just two creatures reaching across the void to share a moment in time.

I looked at the holes in the floor, the wall and the ceiling. That was close.

I called Ava. I went over and took care of her needs. Afterwards, I sat up and said, "I've got to prepare for a meeting."

"Yeah, me too," she said.

I went home and showered. I called Beatriz and went over and took care of her. As I was getting ready to leave, I said, "Will I see you tonight?"

"Yes, of course," she said. "I'll meet you at the bar."

When I got home, the cats were inside, 12 of them; some I knew, some I didn't. The little seal point had convened a hearing, it appeared. "I said I'm sorry," I said. They stared at me like a jury. "I lost control. I offer you, and all cats, my humble apology. My profoundest love, loyalty and respect always have been, are, and always will be devoted to the cats."

They pondered a long moment. They exchanged eye contact. The seal point stood to attention and led the rest in formal array to the door. I let them out.

I opened the medicine cabinet and took out my last jar of cocaine. I wanted to be sharp. I shook the bottle. It was about a quarter full, or three-quarters empty, depending on how you looked at it. I stood there for quite a while looking at the flaky, sparkly powder. I needed to be focused and sharp, not high and wired. I would need that last quarter ounce for my next long drive to see my supplier. Perhaps just a tiny tweak in each nostril? But that would wear off and leave me flat and dull. I could wait till I got to the restaurant, but then I'd be coming on and potentially distractible. I remembered what my old psych prof said about self-medication, a take-off on the line about the lawyer who represents himself. "The man who self-medicates has a fool for both doctor and patient." I needed to be clear and focused and ready for anything. I don't need drugs, I thought. I am my own best self.

40

I dressed in light, loose linen slacks with deep pockets. My hammerless .32 was designed to slip into and out of a pocket without snagging. A Colt, of course, 1903 model, with blue steel and pearl grips—it was a beaut. It was really more of a collector's item—I paid almost two grand for it, a bit of an affectation I'll admit—but it was in excellent shape and a straight shooter. I put on a guayabera, which is worn untucked, to further obscure my outline, and a pair of sturdy river sandals.

I drove out to the restaurant on the lake. I went around to the side. I stood there at the top of the series of decks and looked the place over. It was packed and happening. I realized it was Diez y Seis. A guy on sax was fronting a salsa band with insane percussion. They were rocking the house. An old hippie chick in tie-dye was float dancing and playing finger cymbals.

I went into the bar. Beatriz was there looking fresh and beautiful in a sun dress that showed off a lot of cleavage and a lot of thigh. I kissed her lightly on the cheek.

"Hey baby," I said.

She seemed a little stiff and looked away.

"They're out here," she said. She led me outside.

We descended a few ramps and stairs, circled around some junipers and scrub oak and came upon a large party at a long picnic table. Johnson sat at one end with three tough-looking hombres. At the other end was a bevy of women.

Beatriz showed me to a seat with the men. She went and took her place with the women.

"Howdy, boy" said Johnson. He was laughing. He looked like a farmer in his stained khaki pants and shirt, like he didn't give a shit, like LBJ when he was drinking himself to death but with an extra 150 pounds.

"I've been wanting to see you," he said. "Mighty nice to see you."

"Nice to be here," I said, "with such a fine, mainstream American."

He laughed like he got the irony, but he only got half of it. He pulled out a cigar, stuffed it in his face, lit it, took a couple of puffs and let it go out.

"Hear about that cluster-fuck in Jewell?" he said.

"I saw something on the news," I said.

"I don't believe it was on the news," he said.

"I must have read it in the paper. Some amateur hit two banks."

"Why do you say amateur? I'd say he was damn good."

"Just lucky."

"Maybe not," he said.

He looked down the table toward the women.

"Where's Mary?" he said.

The women looked at each other. "She went to the restroom," Beatriz said. "I'll go get her." She went up the stairs behind the brush.

"These here gentlemen," Johnson said, "represent the Austin Police Department, the Travis County Sheriff's Department and the Texas Department of Public Safety." One black and one white, both heavy, were sitting across the table, and a buff-looking Mexican was next to me on the bench. None of them flicked an eyelid or said a word.

"My friends in law enforcement, they don't mind at all the kind of well organized and well planned business I conduct. They appreciate the professionalism, as long as they derive their benefits, don't you boys?" They stared at me stone-faced. "But they don't like it when this kind of thing spills out into the public. Someone could get hurt, and that makes them look bad. They're a prideful fraternity."

Beatriz came back. Following her was Ava. They sat among the women. I stared at Ava like what the fuck but she wouldn't meet my eye. I looked back at Johnson.

"So you're going to throw me over," I said.

He laughed. "Aw, hell no, boy. I like you."

"What then?"

He kept laughing till he stopped. He was one mean- and ugly-looking son of a bitch. "Yeah, I've seen the tapes," he said. "That Ed. What a comedian."

I looked at Ava. She was looking at me now. All I could do was shake my head. She shrugged. "Sorry," she said.

I looked at Beatriz. Her eyes were full of sorrow and suffering.

"Yeah," he said, "I've known old Mary a long time, employed her services from time to time. I like to work with people I know, people I know I can trust." He grinned. "I can use a fellow like you. Someone kind of half-crazy, but not all the way crazy, you know, someone who can get organized and follow through, but who is ready to go there, right now, without the slightest hesitation, go all the way there if he has to. Yeah, I got a lot of plans for you, boy. You're gonna make me a lot of money."

"I'm retired," I said.

He laughed really nasty. "Not no more you ain't," he said. "And no more of this freelance shit. I can't risk you on anything penny ante. But you'll work and when I say. I got them tapes. I own you, boy."

"Like hell," I said.

I shot Ava in the ear. She was looking away, so, mercifully, she never saw it coming. After all, we had something once.

I knocked off the two cops across the table like bottles on fence posts, one each in the forehead. Don't tell me a .32 is too small when you have one in your brain.

The cop on my right was trying to grapple me with his left hand while going for his gun with his right. I leaned into him. Johnson was struggling to stand. I gave him one in the gut and sat him down. I jammed the muzzle in the cop's ribs but he twisted hard and I shot him in the right elbow. His arm went limp. He stood clumsily drawing his piece with his left hand. I gave him a shove and went over the table. He fired off half a dozen rounds in half a second. I rolled over, came up and popped him center mass. He staggered and kept on shooting wild. I took good aim and hit him in the right eye. That took the fight out of him.

An eerie quiet settled in. I stood there catching my breath.

"I own this place," Johnson said. "We can clean this mess up. I ain't hurt bad. Don't do anything stupid, boy."

I smiled.

"I guess you already did," he said.

I shot him in the temple. The bullet never came out the other side. He slumped in his chair.

I heard the women crying. I turned. Beatriz sprawled on the deck like she was exhausted from making love. I knelt at her side. There was blood on her dress. Her eyes flickered. "I love you," she said. Her eyes closed and she breathed her last.

A tear came to my eye. I stood and surveyed the scene. The light was in the sky, but it was dark down here on earth. I descended the decks to the edge of the cliff and stepped into space.

41

I plunged into the pool. I sank to the bottom. I pushed off and easily rose to the surface and set out swimming.

I took off my shirt. I took off my pants. I had my swim trunks underneath. I swam beneath the rising moon and distant stars. After a while, I let go of the gun and let it sink.

I swam easily and lazily. I dogged it. In the distance, I heard sirens. I swam and floated and loitered. The moon and stars floated peacefully far above. I think I had never before felt so free. Five miles downstream, I came within sight of the dam. I scrambled out onto the rocks and climbed to the roadway.

I started walking.

Of course, I couldn't go home. Every cop and every criminal in the state of Texas would be looking for me.

I thought of the cash in the dresser drawers—almost half a million dollars. I thought of the guitars, resting quietly in their cases. I thought of everything I owned, and I didn't regret a thing. I let it all go.

I thought of the cats with a pang. I would miss them. But cats are a large tribe. Cats are resilient. Cats are self-reliant. Cats can go anywhere. I didn't have to worry about them.

I thought of Ava. I loved her, in my way. She was the only woman I ever wanted to marry. She didn't deserve to die like that. She should never have betrayed me. I thought of the pressures she must have been under and the stress she must have felt, and I forgave her. I let her go.

Beatriz I loved in my way. Maybe I loved her more, maybe less. Who can weigh or measure love? I couldn't take her with me, even if the bullet hadn't found her. I had to let her go.

I felt nothing but compassion for any of them, for the pain and vulnerability that led them to their fate. I was in no way responsible for any of this.

Strangers I met along the way, they gave me clothes. They fed me when I was hungry, they healed me when I was sick.

Drawn as if by some greater power, I followed the rivers and found the ideal home in Galveston.

Seawall Boulevard fronts the Gulf with a brave façade of luxury and fun, hotels, restaurants and tourist traps, all a bit desperate and tawdry. But I have nothing to do with any of that. I live below the seawall, right on the beach.

I lay out the chaise lounge I salvaged from a dumpster behind a motel, and I have all the comforts of home. For a mattress, I have five layers of folded cardboard. Each night I am lulled to sleep by the hush and whisper of the waves. The bugs and birds are part of the deal. If I don't sleep, I watch the play of starlight on foam, the sparkle and dance of phosphorescence, and it's better than any television.

My hair is past my shoulders, a wild tangle of dreadlocks, and my beard covers my chest. My skin is the color of mahogany. I wear a loincloth made from old rags. I have a blanket someone left behind on the beach, and a plastic tarp I found in the dunes, for when it's cold and rainy, which it never is. One stormy night I slept in a culvert, and I was fine.

I know I have money stashed in various accounts, but I can't even remember those old identities. I don't need money. I live like a king. I am well attended, by pelicans, gulls, terns, herons and sandpipers. The beach is alive with crustaceans and insects, and the water is frothy and thick with living creatures, so I'm never lonely.

My best companions, my boon companions are the cats.

In vain attempts to dam the flow of the longshore drift of a barrier island, little humans, in their pride, have freighted huge blocks of billion-year-old pink granite quarried from the hills outside Austin to pile up and form jetties jutting way into the Gulf, which only hastens the erosion of the sand. An unintended consequence, the crannies and crevices of the rocks are inhabited by thousands of cats. Cats of every color and configuration swarm and pour among the boulders with every heave and surge of the waves. They stalk, they pounce, they arch and curl and sleep upside down in the sun.

At first they were a bit standoffish, but then the little seal point showed up. She looked me over pretty good, like this was a different look for me, but she recognized me all the same. She went to the nearest jetty and held a confab, and soon the word had spread to all the colonies and now I am accepted wherever I go.

A thousand miles of water stretch out in front of me, but freshwater can be hard to come by. I sneak around behind buildings and backyards to find an unguarded faucet, and I drink from the hose or straight from the tap.

In the restaurants on the boulevard you can pay 50 bucks for a fish, but I need none of that. I have the entire abundance of nature laid out before me like a smorgasbord—for free. Humanitarians, in their concern for the cats' welfare, in their worry that cats can't take care of themselves (!), every night leave out hundreds of cans of premium cat food. Salmon, chicken, lamb and beef—the cats kindly share their abundance. I take all I need, and I'm eating better than I ever have.

The days roll on, each exactly the same. The sun rises and sets. The tides come in and out. Every moment is the present. And I am free.

About the Author

John Herndon is a poet and filmmaker who lives in Austin, Texas. He has published five books of poetry. Frame Switch, a feature-length experimental thriller based on his screenplay, will be in festival release in 2016. He currently teaches literature and writing at Austin Community College. This is his first novel.

Author Website: johnherndonauthor.com

Made in the USA
Charleston, SC
15 February 2016